"RYAN, WAKE UP."

Long arms snaked up, wrapping like bands of steel around Kayla, moving suddenly to roll her beneath him, completely immobilizing her. His eyes flashed open as he flattened her with his full weight upon the bed.

"What the hell?" he rasped.

"You . . . you were having a nightmare," Kayla said.

"Was I?" he asked softly.

"I heard you from my room."

"And you came running in here to save me from my demons." His grip tightened. "How thoughtful of you." He made a sound deep in his throat, lowering his mouth to her neck.

"I just wanted to make sure you were all right."

"Well, then," he murmured, working his way up to her ear. "I owe you a thank-you."

"No, really," she managed to say as he tugged on her earlobe. "You don't."

Ryan lifted his head, piercing her with fully alert and awake eyes. "I feel I must show you my gratitude."

"No, really. I'll just go back to bed now and let you get some sleep."

He laughed softly and slid his hips over hers. Her heart pounded. Her blood raced. Her bones had long since melted away.

"Ryan, I—"

Her next words were lost as his mouth crashed down upon hers, matching the storm outside, fury for fury.

WHAT ARE *LOVESWEPT* ROMANCES?

They are stories of true romance and touching emotion. We believe those two very important ingredients are constants in our highly sensual and very believable stories in the LOVESWEPT line. Our goal is to give you, the reader, stories of consistently high quality that may sometimes make you laugh, sometimes make you cry, but are always fresh and creative and contain many delightful surprises within their pages.

Most romance fans read an enormous number of books. Those they truly love, they keep. Others may be traded with friends and soon forgotten. We hope that each LOVESWEPT romance will be a treasure—a "keeper." We will always try to publish

LOVE STORIES YOU'LL NEVER FORGET
BY AUTHORS YOU'LL ALWAYS REMEMBER

The Editors

ULTIMATE
SURRENDER

JILL
SHALVIS

BANTAM BOOKS
NEW YORK · TORONTO · LONDON · SYDNEY · AUCKLAND

ULTIMATE SURRENDER
A Bantam Book / November 1997

ISBN 978-0-553-76326-3

Published simultaneously in the United States and Canada

146684614

For my Moms
and their endless support

PROLOGUE

Photographs don't lie, and this one was no exception. A beautiful woman. Long, flowing red hair. Gorgeous, wide blue eyes. Sweet smile.

Dr. Kayla Davies.

She led a charmed life. A perfect life. As a well-respected physician living in a lovely home that most would die for, she had it good.

Style, wealth, affluence—yeah, she had it all.

Damn her.

Viciously, the photo hit the brick fireplace, glass shattering into a thousand pieces. The photograph itself fell to the floor, ruined.

So she had the perfect life, it didn't matter. It just didn't matter because she was a fraud.

She'd die for that.

ONE

So he was a workaholic. So what? Lots of people were. Ryan Scott doubted *they*'d been put on forced vacation.

Okay, so lots of people didn't happen to be detectives in the child abuse department of the LAPD. They also probably hadn't just closed a very public custody case involving a senator that had ended in the senseless murder of a young child.

Ryan swallowed hard as he navigated the desert highway and forced the gruesome image of the child's abused body from his mind.

Yeah, maybe he could use a vacation.

He'd left his Southern California beach home nearly four hours earlier, headed toward Lake Mead. Not his ideal vacation spot, but it would have to do. The winter desert should have seemed harsh and unforgiving, and maybe it was. But to Ryan, who hadn't seen much besides the inside of his unmarked squad car and a courtroom in over three months, it seemed like a glorious, wide-open heaven.

The mountains bled red from the setting sun, dropping huge shadows across the dips and valleys below.

White streaks of narrow clouds marred the bright blue sky. Ryan shoved up his sunglasses and soaked it all in, taking his first deep breath since the day the previous week when he'd stumbled across his grisly find in Senator White's garage.

He forced his eyes to stay steady on the road and his breathing to stay even. He needed this, he thought, as his hands shook slightly. He really needed this.

When he turned off the highway and onto the narrow, deserted road that would take him around the lake toward his final destination, he took the detour he knew he should have taken a long time ago.

Three minutes later he stood in the stark cemetery, looking down at his wife's headstone. His wife, the woman who'd been so desperately needy, so hopelessly obsessive that she couldn't trust or love another soul. She'd also been spoiled, manipulating, and cruel. But he'd harbored the anger and resentment long enough.

The sun hitting his shoulder, and the lake far off in the distance to his north, Ryan stared down at the grave that until then he'd never visited.

I forgive you, he thought, kneeling to rub a finger over the letters of her name. Lauren Davies Scott. In the desert a lone bird chirped. "I don't know if I'll ever forget, but I really do forgive you."

He fell silent, and the huge valley around him seemed to respect that silence. There wasn't a sound. His sigh bounced off the high canyon walls as he rose. "I just hope you can forgive me for not loving you the way you wanted to be loved." With one last look he turned away and climbed into his car.

With that huge load off his shoulders, he got back onto the road and started to relax.

More canyons surrounded him as he passed the entrance to the Grand Canyon. Far below and off to his right he caught a glimpse of the sparkling blue water that ran off Lake Mead. It wasn't far now.

Maybe a vacation wasn't such a strange idea after all. Maybe he'd even water-ski. He smiled. Then Francine's cabin came into view and the memories slammed home, knocking the air from his lungs.

The last time he'd been there had been the last time he'd seen his wife alive.

His ears popped as he maneuvered his car over the windy passage and down to lake level. He shouldn't have agreed to come. The scent of the water came to him now, that fresh, delicious scent that meant outdoors, no work, and a temporary freedom he didn't know what to do with.

It didn't matter. He shouldn't have come.

Pulling himself out of the car, he stared at the lakefront home where he'd be spending the next week. He hadn't thought being there could still hurt, but he'd been wrong, very wrong.

Making his way toward the narrow set of stairs that led from the dock to the house, he stopped short at the sight of a vaguely familiar woman getting out of a sleek sports car. She looked at the house with all the trepidation he'd felt only a minute before.

She turned, and for an eternal second their gazes met. He recognized her, of course, even with the dark sunglasses covering eyes he knew to be blue and shimmering with repressed anger; even with the large sun hat covering waves and waves of wild red hair. Yes, he knew that face, though they'd seen each other only once, at his wife's funeral. It was Kayla Davies.

His dead wife's sister.

Kayla's feet wouldn't budge, refused to take her up the walk to Aunt Francine's cabin. Silly really, since she'd been on the road now for five hours and was starving. All right, so she was always hungry, but that was no consolation to her rumbling tummy.

Of course, it might have been nerves. She'd had a near miss on the highway not too far back, a crazy driver in a sports car that had nearly run her off the narrow road and down a thousand-foot drop. But most likely it came from nothing more than her surroundings. Kayla hadn't seen her beloved aunt in too long, which might have continued if Francine hadn't all but begged Kayla to come this weekend. Worry for the older woman had brought Kayla out of the nice, neat little cocoon that was her life. It'd dragged her away from the center of her universe—eleven-month-old Lindsay.

Kayla tipped her head back, letting the light wind blow over her face. Already she missed Lindsay with a physical ache.

Opening her eyes, she froze, as all thoughts scattered like the breeze at the sight of the tall man standing a few feet from her. Ryan Scott. Without warning, her heart stopped, then started again with a fierce, heavy pounding. The driving impulse to turn and run was strong, but Kayla had learned courage the hard way and wasn't about to give up now.

Why would he come to the place of his wife's suicide?

His gaze settled on her face with a bland curiosity that didn't fool her. Ryan Scott was a master at hiding his emotions. This man had terrorized her sister, had made her life a living hell, and had pushed her into taking her own life. He was a man to be feared.

Kayla didn't do well with fear. She lifted her chin. "Why are you here?"

His smile was as cold as his hazel eyes, his voice filled with derision aimed entirely at himself. "I don't know what the hell Francine's up to this time, but she got me." He shook his head, looking disgusted, and withdrew his gaze from Kayla to stare moodily at the lake. He muttered a ripe curse beneath his breath before whipping his head back to her. "Or was this *your* idea?"

Kayla stared at him, still in shock from the very unwelcome and terrifying sight of him, from hearing that deep voice slightly accented by what she knew others considered his appealing Southern twang. "*My* idea? What are you talking about?"

"Never mind," he said curtly. "Why are you here?"

She refused to answer that. His gravelly voice had been born to charm, but she was immune to his allure. She still had nightmares about what he'd done to her sister. She couldn't stand this man.

He caught her arm in an almost gentle grip of steel as she whirled to leave. "Wait a minute, Ms. Davies."

"Dr. Davies," she corrected him automatically, yanking her arm from his grasp. "And don't touch me." He couldn't know how that had frightened her in that brief second when she didn't think she could free herself of him. Or maybe he did and he liked that fear. According to Lauren, he got off on scaring people weaker than himself. Thank God she'd left Lindsay home with Tess. "I'm leaving."

"Not yet," he assured her grimly. "Not until I find out what's going on. Francine invited you here?"

She chewed her cheek nervously, trying to put thoughts together. Francine was *friends* with this man? Her fear faded, and in its place came a more even-tempered need to find out what he wanted with her aunt. "Yes."

"Hmmm." He stroked his wide jaw, studying her

thoughtfully. "She's up to something all right. I have to admit, it threw me for a loop seeing you standing there, looking so much like—"

"Move out of my way," she demanded, ripping off her sunglasses. How dare he bring up Lauren, in this spot, in that light, easy manner. She wanted to go to the house and talk to Francine. She couldn't imagine what Francine had needed so desperately, especially since they hadn't seen each other in so long.

"No." His voice was even. "You won't leave, at least not yet anyway. You're a Davies. You won't leave until you get what you came for."

She came to an abrupt halt on the step above him, and though she was taller than average, he still towered over her. "What is that supposed to mean?"

"I think you know," he drawled. "If you're anything like Lauren was, you'll know."

Kayla cringed at the comparison. Lauren had been incredibly beautiful, willowy, and talented, everything a woman would envy. But beneath the surface she'd been incredibly insecure and selfish. No one knew that better than Kayla, but to hear him speak of her in that tone when Lauren was dead and gone didn't seem right.

Kayla had forgiven Lauren long ago for her many infractions. Ryan should have, too, if he'd been human enough. Nothing Lauren had done could have excused his treatment of her. Nothing.

Ryan straightened his wide shoulders and slipped his hands inside his trouser pockets. "Tell me something, *Dr.* Davies Why come here now, after all this time?"

The implications of that stung. "You think I'm here to get something from her."

He didn't need to speak, the answer sat in his hard, knowing eyes.

Anger was a blessed relief to the fear. *"You do,"* she

breathed. "You think that." Hurt, she marched past him and started up the stairs. She had no one to blame but herself. Not even Ryan. Francine meant everything to Kayla. No matter the circumstances, she never should have stayed away so long.

Ryan brushed past her to block her path. "I thought you were leaving."

"You knew I wouldn't. You even said so. Now, please, get out of my way."

He didn't budge. "What do you want from her?"

She lifted her chin, telling herself he couldn't see her shaking in her heels. "Get out of my way or I'll toss you down the stairs."

He smiled at that. "Now, that, sweetheart," he drawled, "I'd like to see you try."

It was that voice she decided, that slow, deep, lazy twang that gave him the charming appeal. Plus, he knew how to use it.

It didn't hurt that he had a tough and ruthless bad-boy look about him, with his thick brown hair, rugged features, and lean body that seemed destined for a fight. His eyes held a wealth of hard-earned knowledge that he wasn't afraid to use, and his wide, generous mouth could flatten an opponent with a few words.

They were both based in Los Angeles, where he enjoyed a high-profile detective position. In the last year or so, he'd specialized in children—locating missing ones and relocating abused ones. The media loved him, not just for his success, but because of the added reputation he had for being a love-'em-and-leave-'em kind of guy, a devastatingly masterful lover filled with incredible sensuality and compassion. Women simply fell at his feet. It didn't matter that he never stayed with any one woman; that just fueled the fire both personally and professionally.

Kayla was convinced Ryan could scare even the most hardened criminal into confessing. Maybe that's why he was so good. Maybe he truly loved terrorizing people. God knew, he'd done it often enough to her sister.

"Are you going to? Toss me down the stairs?" he asked now, his eyes amused but cold.

She was sorely tempted.

But that built body could outmuscle her. Despite his flair and ease in dealing with the masses, Kayla knew exactly how cruel this man could be. She may never have actually spoken with him, or even seen him except from a distance at her sister's funeral, but Lauren had told her enough. Yes, Lauren frequently had twisted the truth to suit her needs, but Kayla had seen the proof of physical violence. Kayla had even believed it enough to tell the authorities, hoping for Ryan's arrest. They'd dropped the case almost immediately. She had no idea if he knew what she'd done, but looking into those icy eyes, she thought he probably did.

"I don't want you to hurt her." Ryan's voice hardened protectively.

Shocked into silence, she could only stare at him. Hurt Francine? She loved Francine. "I'd never hurt her."

A thin voice called to them from the top of the stairs of the beautiful cabin. "Ryan? Kayla?"

Both of them looked up into Francine's hesitant smile, then their gazes met in a silent battle. Ryan nodded curtly, indicating Kayla should precede him. She did blindly, uncomfortably aware of his presence directly behind her as she climbed the stairs.

But one look at Francine, and Kayla forgot her fear of the man behind her. Her aunt looked so wonderfully familiar, so completely endearing that she launched herself into the older woman's arms, hugging her tight.

Francine had unconditionally loved Kayla through thick and thin. With her parents long gone, Kayla had depended on her aunt for years. She had been a healthy, precocious child from the start, and going to boarding school from the age of five hadn't changed that. Francine had sent for Kayla every birthday and holiday—and even in between. Kayla'd never forget it.

"Oh, Frannie," Kayla said, slipping into her childhood nickname for the woman who'd raised her, "I've missed you."

Francine squeezed her with a strength that belied her age, and they rocked each other back and forth. For a minute Kayla felt like a child again, treasured, comforted, and wanted.

Until she remembered the silent man standing so rigid beside her.

"Talking on the phone just isn't enough, is it?" Francine murmured, then pulled back to smile reassuringly into Kayla's confused eyes, taking her hands and holding her gaze. "I love you, Kayla. Trust me, please?"

Francine had never asked anything of her, had only given. So what could she do but nod and fight back the questions?

Francine looked at Ryan with a small smile, completely without guile or premise. "You look mildly annoyed, Ryan."

One corner of his mouth quirked, and to Kayla's amazement, those cold eyes softened. "Never with you, Francine." Then he effortlessly folded her small body in his long arms. He bent his head, whispering something softly into her aunt's ear that had her laughing out loud before she hugged him back tightly.

Kayla practically sputtered in surprise. That they were close both surprised and shocked her. No matter what she'd thought about her sister, this man had hurt

Lauren badly, and it hurt now that Francine had remained in contact. "I don't get it."

Both Ryan and Francine looked at her.

"You know each other."

"Yes, we do," Francine said carefully, pulling out of Ryan's arms. "It means so much that you both came."

Ryan looked at her. "You said it was important. You knew I'd come for you."

"Yes," she admitted, glancing away. "I did."

"Well, then," Ryan said slowly, his voice deep and quiet. "I guess I'm with Kayla. Why?"

"There are many reasons for what I've done," Francine said quietly into the silence. "But this isn't the time or place." She sighed. "I'd like to sit down."

Smoothly, Ryan took her arm and turned her toward the doors. "Let's go inside and you can show me where you want to be."

With love shining in her eyes, Francine patted his cheek gently. "You're so good to me, Ryan. So good. Thanks—"

"No. No more of that now." He shook his head as he carefully led her inside. "You know that's not necessary."

Kayla watched, stunned at the easy and genuine affection between the two. Unsettled and confused, she stood rooted to the stair. How could she reconcile this gentle, amusing, caring man with the one who had so abused her sister? Granted, she had never personally witnessed that abuse, but she really had seen the marks and bruises on Lauren clear enough on the day she'd died. Her sister's manipulative ways had been wrong, but they did not give anyone the right to abuse her.

Francine knew that. So what was going on?

None of it made any sense, and for a brief second a flicker of dread and unease shifted through her. Could she be wrong? Could Lauren really have made up such a terrible lie? The fact it was possible had the dread doubling.

"Kayla?" From the shelter of Ryan's arm her aunt turned and looked at her. "Aren't you coming in?"

Kayla blinked away her memories to find Ryan studying her above Francine, his gaze both mocking and challenging.

Okay, so the man hadn't completely changed his colors. The gentleness, the compassion, it all was an act. It had to be. And if he hurt her aunt, she'd . . . what? Well, she'd be there to stop it, that's what. She couldn't possibly waste her time fearing a man who wouldn't dare hurt her. Not here. "Yes," she said as calmly as she could. "I'm coming in." And if her smile was too bright, too sudden, no one commented on it.

Least of all Ryan, who felt Kayla's glowering intensity; he just didn't understand it. He hadn't asked for this vacation; he would have done anything to avoid it. Including risking refusing orders, if it hadn't been for the urgent phone call from Francine, the one and only person alive who genuinely cared for him. She'd needed him, leaned heavily on him in the past year, and now, it seemed, she needed him again. He couldn't imagine for what.

Since she wasn't a person to make demands lightly, or ask for something she didn't have to have, here he was. Yes, this was definitely the last place he would have chosen to come to. The memories were simply too painful. It'd been a year and a half since Lauren had aborted their baby—the baby he'd wanted so desperately, he'd done anything she'd asked, including marrying her. He'd wanted that baby, but he was ready to understand that she hadn't. He just wished she hadn't disappeared for so long afterward so she could have gotten help.

"You okay?" Francine whispered as they crossed the threshold.

He nodded, for a moment unable to respond as he stepped into the cabin he hadn't seen since the night Lauren had told him she'd gotten rid of his baby. He'd left in a grief-stricken rage, and two days later Lauren had disappeared. She'd shown up long months later, only to kill herself.

Francine was staring at him worriedly.

"I'm fine," he whispered harshly.

The minute Kayla entered the house behind Ryan and Francine, she excused herself. She needed to ground herself, to get comfort in the only way she knew how. She needed to hear Lindsay. And to return the three nonemergency pages from her office. As the youngest triage physician at the medical center, she often had the heaviest and most demanding schedule. Thankfully, she'd traded away her Saturday duty, and because she'd scheduled a leave after Francine's phone call, she wasn't on duty again for four days.

Reaching for the telephone in the foyer, she froze at the sight of the framed picture on the wall of two young girls with their arms wrapped around each other. Kayla and Lauren.

The lump that stuck in her throat was unexpected, as was the bitter regret for wasted life. Lauren and Kayla hadn't spoken often. Lauren had become so emotionally demanding that Kayla had, out of necessity, limited their interaction. From the time Lauren and Ryan met and gotten married, all the way up until Lauren's suicide, the sisters had spoken only once. And that had been when Lauren had found herself pregnant from a one-night stand.

Lauren, though older by several years, had been a perpetual child. She'd always hooked up with a fast crowd, continually met Mr. Wrong, and, consequently, always got pushed around by them.

Ryan had been one of those men.

When Lauren had disappeared for long months, and Ryan had put out the word he was looking for her, Kayla had assumed Lauren had screwed up her marriage and was running.

Then Lauren had showed up—beaten to within an inch of her life and holding a baby. She claimed the baby was from an affair, and that if Ryan found out, he'd hurt her. Horrified by the violence her sister had lived with, Kayla hadn't seen the motivation for lying. She'd believed her sister and she'd assured her she'd keep Lindsay safe. And a secret.

Kayla hadn't planned on Lauren's lying to Ryan about aborting the child. Or on her then committing suicide. But she'd kept Lindsay safe, and in the process had lost her heart to the tiny baby. She'd tried to locate the father, but the birth certificate hadn't listed him. Afraid of what Lauren's husband would do, Kayla had gone against everything she valued; truth and justice. All to protect Lindsay. She'd do it again in a heartbeat if she needed to. She'd have done the same to protect *any* child.

It hadn't been difficult. Kayla had only a few close friends, and family hadn't been an issue. She had no one other than Francine.

Lindsay had simply become Kayla's.

TWO

Dinner proved enlightening.

Ryan pushed his plate away, steepled his fingers together, and, for a reason he couldn't fathom, watched Kayla. She fascinated him, and though he hadn't wanted to admit it, just laying eyes on her had been like a sock in the gut. He'd forgotten how beautiful she was. Her curly hair had been piled on top of her head, but tendrils escaped, framing her glowing face as she spoke to Francine.

If it hadn't been obvious by her stricken expression when he'd drilled her about what she wanted from Francine, it became obvious now. Kayla genuinely loved her.

Well, so did he. And that, he supposed, gave them some common ground. God knew, they wouldn't find it elsewhere.

Francine looked good tonight, and unbelievably healthy for her age. Kayla looked good, too, he admitted, but tight as a drum. Francine acted completely unaware of Kayla's palpable stress, but the detective in him assured him she knew.

"Tell me," Francine said to Kayla with a loving smile. "Did you make it all the way up here without adding to the family?"

"Yes, though I nearly ended up in the bottom of the canyon, courtesy of a very rude, speeding car."

Francine paled. "You—you must be more careful. It's not as safe as it once was out there. Certainly, I hope you'd never stop."

"Not unless I saw someone in need of medical attention."

"Even then," Francine insisted. "Do you carry that mobile phone with you?"

"Yes," Kayla said, frowning at Francine's obvious nerves. "Don't worry, Frannie. I'm careful."

Francine visibly shrugged off her troubled air. "Kayla has a soft spot for anything wounded," she told Ryan. "Dogs, cats, birds . . . anything." Her gaze was thoughtful as it rested on Kayla. "People too."

Kayla blushed, but why, Ryan couldn't imagine. He didn't know Kayla, had never exchanged words with her until that day. But in all the time he'd known Lauren, in all the time he'd struggled to get her to keep their baby, then to get professional help for her emotional and mental problems, Kayla had not once been there for her sister.

Though he knew next to nothing about family life, he felt that families should stick together. And no matter how striking or alluring she was, Kayla had failed Lauren. He took a deep breath and admitted to himself he'd forgiven Lauren today—maybe it was time to forgive the sister as well.

He'd been hard on her earlier, had directed his lingering anger right at her. Wrong as it was, that's what had happened, and now she avoided his eyes and fiddled around, probably hoping for a quick escape. He didn't blame her one bit since he knew exactly how formidable he could be when riled.

With his anger gone, his curiosity found itself tweaked—and there was nothing worse than a curious detective. He could just drop it, he thought, watching Kayla squirm. But he wouldn't. Nope, he was going to satisfy that curiosity and discover what made Kayla tick.

Kayla chewed her cheek, playing nervously with the collar of her blouse, and he found himself studying the soft-looking, silky material—and what lay beneath it. Lauren had always been painstakingly thin, but Kayla was not. Much taller than her sister, she had a well-toned build to her. In fact, she had such a curvaceous figure that he wondered how he'd missed noticing it before.

"So you rescue things," he said conversationally, ignoring her little start of surprise at his direct question.

"Sometimes."

Francine laughed. "More than sometimes. Once I picked her up from boarding school for a long weekend and she spotted a hurt rabbit. Must have been a quarter mile off the road, but she insisted we stop. Imagine the two of us trying to chase down a rabbit that didn't want to be saved."

"Did you ever think of telling me no?" Kayla asked, smiling a little and looking embarrassed. "I think I was all of five years old."

Ryan remembered all too well what it was like to be five and alone. He'd been no stranger to fear or hunger. He shoved the unwelcome memories of the South away.

"There was no telling you no, Kayla." Francine patted Kayla's hand and shook her head. "Not when you set your mind on something. You remember what happened?"

"Of course. We caught that thing, pulled a burr from

its hind leg, and both of us sported bruises for a week for our thanks."

"We saved the bunny's life," Francine corrected her niece. "You were always doing that, even as a child. Now look at you. An emergency room physician." She sighed and smiled. "I'm very proud of you."

Ryan watched Kayla blush again, this time with pleasure. And he couldn't help but pry, because he knew Lauren had never been sent away from home. "You went to school very young."

"I was something of a handful," she said diplomatically.

Which was no reason to send a young, defenseless child away, he thought with unwanted sympathy.

"You just needed attention, honey," Francine said. "And you always got it with me. I loved having you here." Her sharp maternal eyes honed in on Ryan. "You look tired, Ryan. Anyone would be with that job of yours." Her eyes held warmth, understanding. "I saw your last case in the news. I'm so sorry."

He wanted no reminders of the nightmare case, would rather discuss why he'd been called there. But Francine had insisted, now that they were all together, it would keep until tomorrow. "I'm fine, Francine." When her gray eyes remained worried, he added more gently, "Let it be."

"Well, it'll be good for you to get away, anyway." She brightened visibly and turned to Kayla. "Tell me about my grand-niece. How's my darling Lindsay?"

Kayla, who had just taken an unfortunate sip of water, choked. "Fine," she managed to answer, keeping her eyes downcast. Her heart started pounding. Why in the world hadn't this occurred to her? Now everything she loved, everything she ever wanted, could be threatened in a heartbeat if Ryan suspected the truth.

"You're a mother," he said, his eyes sharp and surprised.

She forced herself to look into those green-brown eyes, the ones that reminded her so much of a cat on the hunt, and remain calm. "Yes." Her palms started to sweat.

Purposefully, he glanced down at her finger, conspicuously empty of a wedding ring. "I didn't realize you had a child."

"She didn't," Francine said, pride pouring from her every pore. "My generous-hearted Kayla treated Lindsay at birth, then adopted her because of her tragic background."

Kayla, who could hear the roaring of blood in her ears, was momentarily helpless to stop her well-meaning aunt from blowing everything. Helpless because she couldn't tear her gaze from Ryan, who was in turn staring at her with something she couldn't stand to see. Compassion. Her unease now quadrupled. What kind of an abuser had compassion?

"I see," he said quietly, his eyes never leaving Kayla. "Is she well?"

"She's fine," Kayla said. "Very fine, thank you." Could he tell? Could he imagine the terror she felt right that very minute, knowing if he put together the pieces he'd see the truth right in front of him? He'd know Lauren's secret—and hers.

But it must not have been obvious, maybe because he didn't know the age of the child, maybe because he simply couldn't imagine the truth—that Lauren had never had that abortion. Kayla took a deep breath and held it, staring down into her water.

If Ryan knew that Lindsay was really Lauren's, what would he do? Would he retaliate against that child? If the horror stories Lauren had told her about Ryan and his vicious temper were true, he would. Kayla couldn't—wouldn't—risk it.

Lindsay was hers now, with no one but Kayla to protect her. The poor baby had been through enough in her short life, had been to hell and back during the time Lauren had her.

No, Kayla thought with a desperation she hadn't felt since that night Lauren had brought Lindsay to her, no way would she subject Lindsay to any more terror or hardship.

"I loved the pictures you sent," Francine said into the strained silence. "What a beautiful child she is. I wish you could have brought her."

"She had a cold. She's better off with Tess." Her best friend in the entire world, and the only one she'd trusted with the truth. She took a sip of water.

"A baby, especially one so young, needs lots of care." Francine cut herself off abruptly as Kayla had another coughing fit. "Honey, are you all right?"

"Fine." She coughed and sputtered, her eyes tearing as the water seared down her airway. "Just went down the wrong pipe, that's all."

She nearly started choking again, this time in shock as Ryan leaned over and gently patted her back, stroking a warm hand over her spine. "Take it easy, Doc," he drawled. "There's plenty of water to go around."

And, Ryan thought, *plenty of things going on in that pretty head of hers.* He didn't know what the hell had spooked her, but something had. For a minute her eyes had widened, so painfully blue and stricken, he'd actually looked around for the source of her distress. Her hands still shaking, she placed them on the table and pushed herself up to stand.

"I'm sorry," she whispered, dropping her napkin on

the table and reaching into her pocket to pull out her beeper. "I just have calls to make. That's all."

Ryan stood also, his every nerve on alert. Being the best at what he did gave him an advantage. His gut instincts always proved right. Well, his gut was screaming about instincts now. Something was very wrong. He could feel it. This woman was running from something, or someone. It bothered him to see her so afraid and nervous. "You don't look tired," he ventured to say. "You look upset."

"I—no!" She forced a smile he knew damn well was faked. "I'm not upset, really. Please." She let out a quick breath of air. "Please, sit back down and enjoy your dessert. Both of you. I have a lot of work to catch up on."

She hightailed it out of the room, leaving both him and Francine staring after her. "Poor dear," Francine said softly. "She works too hard, she worries too much. She feels too much."

Ryan nodded. That may all be true, but he'd realized two things—Kayla was not at all what he'd expected, and she chewed her cheek when she felt nervous. Something she'd done every time she'd lied.

He had no doubt, Kayla *had* lied.

What could a poised, well-educated, and most likely very wealthy young woman possibly be hiding?

Kayla picked up the telephone in the darkened kitchen with hands that trembled. Thankfully, there were Twinkies on the counter for later. Nothing like good old-fashioned stress to whet her appetite.

She'd been a heavy kid because of her tendency to eat away her problems, and it was only because of her careful and diligent exercise now—which she hated—

that she stayed at her optimum weight. But being good was a never-ending struggle.

Dinner had been agonizing. She'd eaten everything in sight without tasting a bite. Even now, hours later, she still hadn't managed to talk to Francine alone, but if she had, Kayla hadn't the foggiest notion of what she'd say.

She planned the words in her head: Lindsay is really Lauren's and I adopted her because Lauren begged me to, because one glance at that helpless infant and I fell in love—but when Lauren got herself beat up by her ex-husband and then killed herself, she left me no choice but to protect the baby with my own life.

Everything sounded so jumbled now.

She dialed home and let out a deep breath. Just talking to Lindsay and Tess would relax her enough to fall asleep. She hoped.

"Hello?"

"Tess," Kayla said with relief, her words echoing in the empty kitchen. "Is it too late?"

"Of course not," Tess said, a smile in her voice. "Lindsay's awake, and causing trouble as usual."

Love for the baby came shining through in Tess's voice, and not for the first time Kayla realized how lucky she was. Tess had come to her last year, a nurse deep in the throes of burnout, ready for a change. Kayla had in turn been desperate for someone reliable to watch Lindsay during the day, when she worked at the medical center.

It had been a match made in heaven. Tess and Lindsay had taken to each other just as Tess and Kayla had. The three of them were a family now, and Kayla felt eternally grateful for the care and support Tess provided them both.

"Ask her if she misses me," Kayla said softly, feeling needy.

"You mean since the last time you called, an hour ago?" Tess teased. "Of course she does."

Kayla leaned against the counter, thankful for the dark. It made it easier to picture Lindsay's happy face.

"You okay out there?" Tess asked with concern. "You sound kinda out of sorts."

"I'm fine." How could she explain the mess she'd found herself in? Who knew where Ryan Scott was at the moment, but those unsettling eyes of his had missed nothing at dinner, and the last thing she needed was for him to catch her discussing him.

"Tell Lindsay I love her," she said softly to Tess, closing her eyes against the wave of homesickness that assaulted her. She cared for the ill every day, gave it all she had—her heart, her soul, everything. Sometimes she gave so much, she had nothing left—but then she'd go home and see Lindsay and Tess. They loved her exactly as she was, and the realization of that was every bit as amazing and precious each and every time she thought about it. "I'll be home in a few days."

"We'll be waiting."

Kayla slowly let go of the receiver and stood there a moment, head bent, her heart a heavy weight in her chest.

"You *still* look upset."

She gasped and whirled to find Ryan standing not two feet from her, his eyes so dark and shiny, they looked black. With his dark shirt and trousers, and the shadow from the hallway light over his face, he seemed hard, dangerous, and absolutely, stunningly handsome.

"Your phone call disturbed you."

The man was single-minded. She shrugged, forcing a calm over her racing heart. Why did he have to stand that close? To purposely scare and intimidate her? It wouldn't work. But she had no place to back up to except the countertop. Feeling stifled, she stood her ground, cursing the dark kitchen. Remaining at ease was critical, she reminded herself. He'd been trained to detect any sign, exploit vulnerability, use weakness to his gain. "I told you at dinner, I'm not upset."

"Then why are you wringing your hands?" he asked quietly.

Damn him. "Because I'm not used to pushy men. I'd appreciate it if you'd move out of my way."

"Who were you talking to?"

Why she answered him then, she'd never know. "My daughter."

"And she upset you?"

She hesitated, chewing on her cheek. "I told you, I'm not—"

"You're not a very good liar, Kayla," he admonished her easily, reaching out with one finger to run it over her cheek.

The touch did something to her, she supposed. Maybe it was the easy affection, maybe it was just being touched as she hadn't been in far too long. But the admission came from nowhere. "I miss her."

His jaw tightened and his eyes flickered with sympathy while the irony of the entire situation twisted like a knife inside Kayla. Lauren had told her how this man had wanted a baby of his own. How unfair it seemed that Lauren had not given him a baby, but had had one with someone else—someone Lauren refused to name. But then she forced her heart to harden. This man didn't deserve a baby.

"I'm sorry."

The soft-spoken, genuine words he spoke were the last straw. She pushed past him, needing to escape his suffocating closeness, and quickly walked to the swinging kitchen door, fully expecting him to try to stop her.

He didn't, and she paused to look back.

Standing just as she'd left him, he watched her with those shuttered eyes. On the counter the Twinkies beckoned her, and she wished with all her might she'd grabbed one. Gaining control with difficulty, she turned and rushed up the stairs and down the long hallway to her bedroom.

Leaning back against the bedroom door, she closed her eyes; her pulse raced with fear, with nerves, and with something else she couldn't put into words. She'd gotten herself into scrapes before, she'd made it a lifelong habit, but this one took the cake. Because, for the life of her, all she could think of was her tingling hands, still burning from pushing against Ryan's rock-solid chest, and his quiet gaze. And the compassion brimming from his eyes when she'd told him about Lindsay.

Why did he have to have the most compelling eyes she'd ever seen? And why, oh, why, did he have to be so effortlessly sexy?

She couldn't stay.

Get a grip, she told herself. He's just a man. A man who could hurt her and her daughter, especially if he knew the truth about Lindsay.

Just that thought effectively brought back her terror of Ryan's violent tendencies.

She still vividly remembered the day of Lauren's service, how she'd gone into the funeral parlor's office, hoping to have a quick word with the director. But he hadn't been there, Ryan had. His back toward her, he'd been oblivious of her presence, flipping through a photo album on the desk. In horror, she'd watched as he'd cursed luridly, scooped up the album, and flung it across the room. Terrified, Kayla had run from the room, never to forget the sight of his temper.

She'd do well to remember it now.

———✦———

To Ryan's discomfort, he had the dream.

As always, it undid him. Haunting visions of arms reaching for him, depending on him, needing him. But again he failed, and before he could get a good grasp, the weak, helpless cry was silenced. Forever. Then he'd see a child's body floating facedown in water, drifting away.

Waking frightened and completely powerless was par for the course. But this time the image stayed with him.

It was this house, Ryan realized as he sat straight up in the predawn light, shaky and trembly. This house— the last place he'd seen Lauren. She'd been pregnant here, with his baby. The baby he'd never see or hold.

Swiping a hand over his face, he tried to dispel his lingering fear and horror, knowing he needed to get out of there, away from the memories that had him so shaken. He needed to go home, get back to work. But he had no work, he reminded himself. And there was something else, something he couldn't forget.

Francine needed him. He'd needed her once, too, though he hadn't wanted to admit it at the time, even staunchly denied it, but she'd paid him no heed and had come through for him like no one else ever had before or since. He'd never forget it.

He owed her. He'd stay. Letting himself outside in the early dawn, he ran fast and hard along the lakefront, using the power of his body to cleanse his mind. Not hard, with the view he had. As the sun rose up and over the canyon peaks, it covered the world below in golden splendor. The lake shimmered and sparkled with a thousand stars of light as the first rays hit it.

For some reason, he thought of Kayla and her glorious hair. How when she smiled she lit up like a sunrise. Oh, he was something. *Lit up like a sunrise?* A poet he was definitely not. Good thing he could still laugh at himself.

Pushing himself, he ran harder, his running shoes pounding the dirt path, the sun lighting the way and warming his body. Only when his thoughts cleared and his body quivered with exhaustion did he turn back.

Francine sat at her kitchen table, two cups of steaming coffee in front of her. When he came in, she pushed one toward him, but he shook his head and went to the sink for water. Leaning back against the counter, he looked at her. "What's up?"

"Sit down, honey." He didn't move, and she sighed. "Please?"

He relented with a sigh of his own, straddling a chair. He propped his elbows on the back of it and waited.

"You had a nice run?"

"Compared to the smog-clogged streets of L.A., yeah." He studied her. "You okay?"

"Yes."

"You sure?"

"Yes, Ryan," she answered with a little smile that told him how much his concern meant to her.

He downed the last of his water. "Then tell me what's going on."

She gave him a half smile. "Don't you like her?"

"This isn't high school, Francine. You're up to something, but what, I can't imagine."

"She doesn't like you much." Her eyes clouded. "You're a pussycat at heart, Ryan, you just didn't want her to know that. But I can't figure out why."

"Francine," he said gently, reaching for her hand. "You wanted me here this weekend, and I came. But you know it's difficult for me."

"Yes," she admitted. "I know."

He sighed and stood. "So why? Why am I here? It sure as hell isn't so you can play matchmaker."

She looked down and stared at their joined hands. "Kayla needs you, Ryan."

He'd heard that urgent tone before, though not often. It spelled fear and trouble, and he automatically responded. "Needs me? Is she in some sort of trouble?" Of course she was, he'd smelled it on her. Not only that, she was a Davies, wasn't she? Trouble followed them.

"Yes. But not even Kayla understands how deep she's in it."

Great. So much for vacation. He sat back down, unwillingly hooked. "Dangerous trouble?"

"Definitely."

He watched Francine worry her hands together and felt a twist of irritation. Couldn't Kayla have brought her problems somewhere else? This woman didn't deserve it.

"I'm afraid for her, Ryan. Will you help?"

Okay, so someone wanted to hurt the vulnerable woman he'd met last night. He thought of her child and how she hadn't been wearing a ring. He shouldn't care, didn't want to care. But he did. He told himself it was the cop in him, that's all. "What is it? A boyfriend? Ex-husband? Old patient?"

"There is no husband," Francine said, and the quick spurt of relief that shot through him only further annoyed him. "There was a fiancé a couple of years back. He got rough and she dumped him. There's been no man since—she's sworn off them. After her experience, I don't blame her."

Ryan's hands tightened on the edge of the table as the all-too-familiar rage filled him. He'd never understand or forgive the needs of certain men to overpower women, or anyone for that matter, by aggression and force. He saw it nearly every day on his job, yet he'd never managed to toughen his heart against it. Physical violence still made him sick.

"I thought you haven't seen her since . . . Lauren's death."

"We keep in touch on the telephone." Francine stood, refilled her coffee, and turned, her face filled with worry and sorrow. "I found one of Lauren's diaries last week, Ryan. It was here, left or forgotten, I don't know which."

His stomach clenched. "Burn it."

"I read it," she admitted. "And I think both you and Kayla should read it."

"Not me," he said firmly. "The past is over and done."

Francine looked at him. "It's the very thing Kayla said when I told her on the telephone."

So they agreed about something.

"I'm very afraid for Kayla, Ryan," Francine said quietly.

"Why?"

Francine turned away. "Can't you just protect her for me?"

He shook his head. He wouldn't do this, absolutely not. "You've asked me for my help, but you won't tell me what exactly you need?"

"I'm sorry," she whispered, gripping her mug with white knuckles. "I can't break my confidence. I'm all she has, it would destroy her to know I've told you." She hesitated. "I wouldn't ask you to do this for me if it wasn't so important."

He had no choice, really, no choice at all. He glanced out the window, struggling. The sun had risen in all its autumn glory now, shining bright on the ground. He could see the lake, waiting. So much for his visions of relaxing and maybe even getting out on the water. "Just when is she going to tell me what she needs?" he asked wearily.

"You've got to make her trust you first."

"What if she still won't tell me?"

"You can't push her. Eventually she'll come to you because she won't have a choice." She took a breath. "But if she doesn't by the end of your trip, I'll tell you everything. I'll have to."

"Look," he said in a last-ditch effort to get out of this. "I'd do anything for you. I love you. But . . . well, I was married to her sister, for God's sake."

"I know," she said softly, coming to him and laying a hand on his shoulder. "Lauren just about destroyed you, I *know* that, more than anyone else, I know." Her words were gentle, her eyes bright. "But you'll do this anyway. For me. Because you know I wouldn't ask you if I didn't have to."

"Yeah." He rubbed his eyes and ignored the sudden ache in his chest. "I'll do this—for you."

The day dawned as Kayla sat on the dock, watching the swells of rough water slap against the side of Francine's boat.

She sat, waiting and wondering. Waiting until Francine woke up, and wondering what it was she needed from her. Worrying about being away from Lindsay and work. She'd been sitting there when Ryan had jogged past her, and despite herself, she'd stared, mesmerized by the sight. With each stride, his running shorts shifted high on his taut thighs, leaving little to her imagination. Not that she needed one with Ryan. The white T-shirt he wore clung to his defined chest, damp with sweat. Every muscle on that tight body worked hard and efficiently.

He looked like a sun-bronzed god.

Except for his tense eyes. She was thankful not to know what he'd been thinking.

The sun came up and over the canyons surrounding her. Her stomach growled in the quiet morning, reminding her she had yet to eat breakfast. The cookies she'd sneaked down for in the middle of the night weren't going to hold her over much longer.

After a few minutes, two figures, shadowed by the sun directly behind them, came from the house, one tall and broad, the other small and dainty. The closer they came, the more detail she could see. And her frown deepened. Francine's smiling face didn't quite hide her worry or her love. Ryan's unsmiling face showed neither. He looked at her grimly, and Kayla got the message quite clearly.

She wasn't going to like this.

"Here you are," Francine said a little too brightly. "I need your help, honey."

"Okay," she said uneasily. The wind kicked up and Kayla pulled her thin sweatshirt closer to her, shivering despite the sun. Dressing in her favorite old college clothes had seemed like a luxury after her endless white doctor coats, but now she was wishing she'd added a heavier sweater.

"Cold?" Ryan asked. He reached for the zipper on his sweatshirt as if to take it off.

"No!" she said quickly. "I'm fine." She rubbed her nervous, damp palms on her ratty jeans, feeling nothing but irritation that Ryan could make his faded, threadbare jeans look so mouth-wateringly right on that built body, while she felt so rumpled and shabby. "Francine," she murmured, "we need to talk."

"Of course, but I was hoping you'd help the sick duck first."

"Sick duck?"

Her aunt held up a small bag. "Hopefully, you'll find everything you need in here. Here's the boat keys."

She glanced at Ryan. He raised his eyebrows, looking innocent. As if that were even possible. She smelled a conspiracy. "Francine—"

"She *limps*, Kayla. Can you imagine the poor thing trying to survive here, like that?"

"But—"

"Oh, be a sport, Kayla, save the duck."

She glanced at Ryan and saw the challenge in his eyes. Francine watched her expectantly.

"I'll go find the duck," she said quietly.

"I knew you wouldn't let her suffer," Francine said happily.

"No, we can't let her suffer." Kayla couldn't stand to think about any person or animal suffering. It was one of the things that made being a doctor so terribly painful as well as satisfying. She had to see the pain in others before she could begin to heal it. "Where did you see her last?"

"Across the inlet. She swam away and I didn't see her come back."

Kayla climbed in the boat, looking across the narrow inlet where they sat to the major waterway. The boat rocked and she jerked around to see Ryan standing behind her. Her heart sank.

He was going with her.

THREE

"What are you doing?" Kayla demanded. She dropped the supplies to a seat and stared at Ryan, dread filling her.

"I'm going with you."

That low voice with the slight southern twang was *not* going to persuade her. "No, you're not."

He moved forward, taking the keys from her limp hand. "Don't be ridiculous, Doc. You can't possibly drive the boat, look for the duck, *and* catch it all by yourself."

She sure could try. "I'll be fine." But he'd already started the boat.

The sudden momentum had Kayla sinking to a seat. Sitting up, she nearly jumped out, but she hesitated a second too long and then they were moving too fast. With no choice but to accept her fate, she gritted her teeth and tried not to panic.

As the shore got farther and farther away, she plopped back gracelessly in her seat. Dammit. Ryan's back was to her, his long legs planted far apart, his shoulders impossibly wide and set, his hands steady on the controls. She could just picture his cocky grin and mocking curved eyebrow. His laughing eyes. She rolled hers. A regular modern-day pirate he was. Then he glanced at her with a serious intensity she knew matched her own. For a moment she couldn't look away. Her stomach muscles danced, and still they stared.

He looked away first.

Kayla blinked, startled that he'd drawn an emotion from her that had nothing to do with fear. Man, she needed cookies.

Food was just about the furthest thing from Ryan's mind. He drove the boat hard and fast, enjoying the cool air on his face and the occasional icy drop of water on his arms. Here, at last, was the freedom and peace of mind he'd craved.

Except, of course, for the silent woman behind him.

"There she is." He pulled back on the throttle and let the boat idle. The duck was clearly visible on a small jut of land twenty-five feet ahead.

Kayla came up beside Ryan, frowning with concern. "Oh, look," she whispered. "She's cradling her leg. Poor thing."

Kayla's sharp eyes had narrowed critically on her patient; her hands settled on her hips in a position of authority. Like the night before, her hair threatened to fall from its sort of endearing, if not precarious, lopsided perch on top of her head. The sweatshirt she wore had been zipped to the seductive spot between her breasts, repeatedly drawing his attention there, the T-shirt beneath snug enough to perfectly outline her lush curves. Those faded jeans of hers emphasized her waist and hips in interesting ways, and once again Ryan felt struck by the physical difference between Kayla and her sister.

Lauren had been so proud of that scrawny body he'd always thought was too skinny. She'd ridiculed Kayla repeatedly, insinuating she was fat. In fact, Kayla was just about the furthest thing from fat Ryan had ever seen, but he could see why Lauren had felt threatened. Many women would be intimidated by that curvy yet tight body. Disturbing as it was, he could hardly keep his gaze off her.

"Hope I can catch her," she murmured, pulling on a pair of gloves she'd found in the bag.

"We will." He reached in for the other pair of gloves.

Kayla stared at him, seemingly startled as her lips parted in surprise. "You're going to help?"

Insanely, he wondered if she liked to kiss—she had such a perfectly kissable mouth with those wide, full lips—or if, like her sister, she only pretended. "Yeah, I'm going to help." He yanked on a glove. "Did you think I would just stay on the boat and supervise?"

"Actually, yes."

Pulling on the second glove, he shook his head, inexplicably disappointed. "That's not very flattering, Kayla."

"I didn't mean it to be."

He couldn't see her eyes behind the mirrored sunglasses she'd put on, but he had no trouble sensing her hostility. "What's the matter with you?"

She pushed her hair from her face, then played with the zipper on her sweatshirt, avoiding his gaze.

Why did she seem suddenly panicky and nervous? Was she frightened about the mysterious danger Francine had hinted about?

"Do you have a problem, Kayla?"

"It seems to be you." She looked at him suspiciously

and lifted her shoulders. "Why are you here? Why are you trying to help me? What do you want?"

How easy it would be to tell her that her aunt had asked him to help her, but she wasn't ready to hear that. The boat dipped and swayed gently in the soft swells as he said carefully, "I'm just trying to help you save the duck."

She looked at him, and even with the sunglasses he easily read her mistrust and disbelief. He laughed shortly and rubbed his eyes. How was he supposed to help this temperamental, moody woman? And had he really promised Francine he would? "Can we do that?" he asked, looking at her. "Just save the duck?"

She searched his face for God knew what, and eventually she nodded slowly. "Okay." She yanked her sweatshirt off, mumbling to herself as it caught on her arm. He didn't dare make a move to help, not wanting to touch her and set her off further. She tossed the thing down to the seat behind her, still muttering.

"You're really a prize in the mornings, Kayla," he ventured to say lightly. "You always so cheerful? Or is it just me?"

She spared him a glance. "I'm just surprised you're going to help."

Her quick judgment rankled. "Why? It's not like you know me. We've never even exchanged words before yesterday."

Slowly, she removed her sunglasses, confusion and wariness warring in her eyes. Again she subjected him to a lengthy, silent look. Then apology lit her eyes. "You're right," she admitted. "And I'm usually not so disagreeable, but . . . well, I'm hungry."

"You're hungry."

"Yeah." Her lips curved. "Starving, actually. I always am. It's a curse."

He found himself smiling back. Her admission seemed unexpectedly sweet. "Let's catch us a duck. And then you can dip into the goodies Francine packed."

"She packed— Of course she did." With a sigh of resignation, Kayla moved beside him as he drove the boat forward until it glided close to shore.

The duck hobbled backward, watching suspiciously as Ryan jumped down to the shallow water, then pulled the boat farther up on the shore to secure it. "Come on, Doc. The duck's waiting." He lifted a hand up to Kayla.

She jerked back from his sudden move.

"What the hell?" He stared at her, seeing the brief flicker of fear before she managed to hide it behind a mask of indifference. It all happened so fast, he couldn't be sure of anything, except that she didn't want him to touch her. "Kayla?"

She merely shook her head, and without a word jumped to the beach by herself.

Remnants of fear from her previous relationship, he wondered as he followed her, or something else?

Kayla couldn't have told him, her emotions were too mixed up, too conflicted. Ryan wasn't acting as a man prone to violent tendencies should. No, he was almost . . . sweet. Caring. And far too attractive. It became easy to use the duck as an excuse to ignore the man next to her.

"Here, now," she cooed softly to the duck staring at her uneasily. "I'm not going to hurt you." She took another step toward the duck, then another, pleased at her progress. But just as Kayla reached down for her, the duck spread its wings and honked noisily, flapping backward a good ten feet. With a good-natured shrug Kayla tried again. Then again.

Five minutes later she had to admit the duck didn't want to be caught. She glanced at Ryan, who stood close to the edge of the shore, his arms crossed, looking amused.

"Finished yet?" he asked in that smooth drawl of his.

She lifted a brow at his unbearable smugness. "If you can do better, I want to see it."

"Fine." Quietly, purposefully, he stalked the duck, his expression even and intent. His gaze met the duck's, and he never wavered as he walked right up to the quivering thing and scooped it close to his chest, cradling it in his big hands.

Amazed, Kayla moved closer in time to hear him whisper softly, "That's it, darlin', just stick with me. The doc here'll patch you up in no time." The duck jerked, her eyes wide with fear, but Ryan just stroked a soothing hand over her ruffled feathers. "Don't fret now," he said in that seductive voice that had Kayla's stomach doing a slow roll. "You'll be all right just as soon as the doc gets a look at you." Unbelievably, the duck settled against him trustingly.

Over the duck's head he grinned cockily at her. "See?"

She ignored him and bent toward the duck, not wanting to think about the ease with which he'd charmed the animal. Or her. It was that drawl, she told herself. It should be illegal to have such a husky voice coupled with the rest of that sexy package that made up Ryan Scott. The combination would be lethal to any woman.

He didn't say a word while she removed a piece of glass from the web of the duck's foot. No doubt some camper had thoughtlessly left the glass on the sand. Ryan worked quietly and efficiently alongside Kayla while she cleansed the wound, saving her more than once from being bitten by holding the duck's head. Through it all, he chatted to the duck, trying to calm the bewildered animal.

By the end, the duck wasn't the only one distracted.

Kayla plopped on the sand and watched the duck check out its cleaned cut, uncomfortably aware of Ryan standing slightly behind her.

The water lapped noisily at her feet. Birds chirped loudly, hoping for a handout. But for once the beauty of her surroundings completely escaped her.

She'd come to the disturbing conclusion that Ryan might not be the monster she'd been led to believe. She hated to be wrong about anything, but she knew she couldn't let simple pride stand in the way of something so critical.

She almost . . . liked him.

The duck, restless by now, straightened slowly and waddled toward the water's edge, hardly favoring the injured leg at all.

Kayla tucked in her knees and rested her forehead on her bent legs. It would be a good thing if Ryan wasn't who she'd thought, wouldn't it? It would mean she had no reason to fear him.

She nearly leapt out of her skin when he touched her shoulder.

"Hey," he said quietly, dropping down lithely beside her. "Just me." He handed her a croissant from Francine's bag. "You look ready for a break."

"Thanks." She tried to smile as she ate, but it was difficult with those piercing eyes on her.

The duck swam gingerly, though close to shore. "She looks fine, thanks to you," he said easily.

He sat so close, she could count the golden specks in his eyes, see every character line on his chiseled, rugged face. He popped his last bite into his mouth, chewing slowly. She watched his throat muscles contract . . . and again her stomach muscles danced. She hadn't wanted another man in so long, she almost didn't recognize the feelings and symptoms of sweaty palms and light-headedness. Stupidity. She felt every one of those things now. She was absolutely crazy to allow herself to be attracted to this man.

She had to make a decision, and quickly. Did she trust him? A quick, haunting vision of Lauren's battered body, the same body she'd been forced to identify for the police, flitted through her mind, making her shiver in the early morning light despite the warm sun at her back.

"Want to talk about it?" he asked softly.

She'd alerted the cop in him, she could tell by his sudden stillness. "No," she whispered.

He sighed and looked over the water to the far shore, where Francine's cabin sat, though they couldn't see it. "Look, I'm sorry I was rude yesterday. Truth is, being here again sort of took me off balance. I lashed out at you, and it was wrong."

He'd lashed out. Something he was used to doing? She found herself scooting away from him just for distance, and for the first time in three years gave her ex-fiancé a thought.

At the time, Kayla had thought it was true love. But they'd fought constantly over her demanding career. When he'd actually "lashed out" and slapped her one night in a rage, she'd been smart enough to bail. She'd never looked back.

"Do you forgive me, Kayla?" Ryan asked in a low voice, sounding alarmingly sincere. She hesitated, running warm sand through her fingers.

A gentle but firm hand lifted her chin, forcing her to meet his gaze. His eyes held regret, sweet enough to make her eyes close against the onslaught of unwanted emotions.

"Do you?" he asked again, still holding her face in his caressing fingers.

Before she could comment, her former patient vivaciously kicked up her heels, splashing Ryan with a steady stream of icy lake water.

Gasping, they both leapt to their feet. Ryan stood there, his soaked sweatshirt clinging to him, showing off muscle and wiry strength. Her gaze flew up to his face as the breath backed up in her throat, uncomfortably aware of him as a man. But then she caught sight of a drop of water hanging off his nose.

It must have been the tension, but it struck her as hysterically funny.

At her muffled giggle, his eyebrows came sharply together. "Are you laughing at me?"

She nodded helplessly. She'd cracked for sure, she thought wildly, but she couldn't help it. She slid back down to the sand, holding her mouth to contain her laughter.

In one fluid motion he yanked her up in his arms, shifted her tight against his chest, and strode directly into the water until he stood in the lake up to his calves.

At first Kayla could only gape up at him, in shock at the unexpected contact of their bodies. But when his intentions became clear, she unthinkingly threw her arms around his neck. "Don't you dare!" she threatened. "Or I'll—"

"You'll what?" A small smile played about his mouth as he leaned his head alarmingly close to hers, waiting patiently.

One of his arms was wrapped beneath her knees. The other was around her back. The fingers of one hand touched her ribs, just beneath her breast. The air backed up in her throat. Speaking wasn't an option. Closing her eyes, she held tight and tried not to feel the impressive bulk of muscles beneath her fingers.

His warm breath tickled her face. "I wonder . . ." He pretended to drop her, then caught her effortlessly, inches from the water.

She hoped her considerable size strained his arms. "You're going to be very sorry," she promised, ruining the threat by squealing when he did it again.

With his arms surrounding her, his wet sweatshirt soaking her, and his face unnervingly close, Kayla forgot to be afraid. She forgot to analyze her feelings. All she could think was, his damp skin smelled clean and very male. His warm body felt good against hers. He was— Oh, God.

He was her sister's husband.

Her arms fell from around Ryan's neck as the urge to play fled. "Put me down. Please."

Watching her, he took his arm from beneath her knees so that her body slid down slowly over his wet, hot one . . . directly into the water.

"Oh!" she cried as the cold water seeped up to her knees. Awkwardly, she splashed out of the water and looked down at her soaked tennis shoes and jeans.

"You told me to." He shrugged innocently as he came out of the water.

She narrowed her eyes on the man whose mouth quirked with amusement and mischief. She returned his guileless smile and walked slowly toward him. "You're right," she said sweetly. "And it's very good of you to follow my directions so concisely." Directly in front of him now, she said conversationally, "So many men can't follow directions, you know."

He opened his mouth, but she lunged, using the one and only martial arts move she'd mastered.

Ryan lay flat on his back in the sand before he could say a word.

Kayla backed up quickly, but she needn't have worried. Ryan didn't move a muscle, just stared thoughtfully up at the sky. Finally, she couldn't stand the suspense. "Ryan?"

"Hmmm?"

"Aren't you going to get up?"

"Do you know any more moves like that one?"

"Yes," she lied.

"Then I don't think so," he said, very still.

Flooded with remorse, Kayla took a step forward. Maybe she'd hurt him and he was too proud to admit it. Gingerly, she came closer. "Are you all right?"

He closed his eyes and didn't answer.

"Ryan?" The doctor in her took over. She squatted next to him and touched his arm. "You're hurt—"

She finished her last word from her bottom in the sand, where he'd put her after moving with lightning speed, knocking her gently and completely flat.

"Oh, I'm fine," he assured her, grinning cockily from his stance far above her.

"Very funny." Sand clung to every inch of her wet clothing. She stilled, realizing she'd just laughed, carefree as she pleased, with the man she'd lived in fear of for the last year of her life.

"Oh, look at that," Ryan suddenly said in a hushed, reverent tone. He grabbed her shoulders and turned her out to the water. There she saw the duck—and her five little ducklings wading along behind her.

"Oh, they're precious," she whispered, experiencing the familiar thrill of victory. It mattered not one bit that her last patient had been just a duck. "Isn't it lovely?"

"Yes," he said, his voice husky as he stared down at her. "So lovely."

Suddenly aware of how close he stood behind her, his hands on her shoulders, his chest and legs lightly brushing against her back and thighs, a strange set of emotions swirled inside her. Fear and . . . what? Lust? She hoped not, but she wasn't one to deny facts. He both attracted and repelled her.

And he thought her lovely.

She stepped away and he let his hands fall. His gaze roamed over her, landing on her untamed hair, then her wet face. It heated when he got to her very wet T-shirt, then lowered to her soggy feet. Strangely enough, that caught his utmost attention.

"Your feet are drenched."

"No kidding?"

He shook his head, frowning. "That was thoughtless of me. Let's go back. You'll catch a cold."

She wanted to assure him that was only a myth, that she stood more chance of catching a cold from touching him than from her wet feet. But she didn't because she wanted to go back. Didn't she?

She needed to think, needed to be alone, because this fun, caring, gentle side of Ryan Scott completely conflicted with everything she believed of him.

"Why do you do that?"

She started at the question. He'd moved closer to her, their arms nearly touching as they stood side by side. "Do what?"

"Shut me out of your every thought."

"Do I do that?"

"You know that you do." He turned toward her and gently pulled on her arm until she faced him. "What I want to know is why."

Those eyes mesmerized her, demanded things she couldn't—wouldn't—give. "I don't know you," she said, struggling with her mounting panic that had nothing to do with fearing him. "So why would I want to share my every thought?"

"I'd settle for some of those thoughts," he said seriously, though one corner of his mouth tilted up. "After all, we *are* related."

"*Were!* As in the past tense," she cried softly, the reminder of that like a two-fisted punch. "Lauren is dead."

"Yes," he said quietly, his gaze hooded as he gave nothing of his own thoughts away. "She's quite dead."

She had to ask, had to know, it was like a sick need welling within her. "Ryan, would you—could you tell me about your marriage?"

He hesitated, watching her. "Why do I get the feeling you've already heard about it?"

"Lauren told me a little," she admitted. Something, probably a flicker of the fear she was beginning to feel, gave her away.

"Did she?"

At his dangerously quiet voice, she backed up a step. His eyes darkened even more at the fearful move. "Hmmm. I bet that was good. And you believed it." He laughed when she flinched. "This entire time you've been afraid, not of something I don't understand, but of *me*. God."

She couldn't answer. Her mouth simply wouldn't work as she watched him get angrier and angrier, and the fear she'd been holding at bay threatened to overwhelm her.

"Haven't you?" he demanded, reaching for her, holding her shoulders.

She flinched again at his touch, though it was gentle and unrestraining. "Yes," she whispered, "Yes."

"How dare you." The words were soft. Deadly. "You've tried and convicted me on the word of a liar."

He grimaced in understanding. "It was you. You're the one who started that investigation against me, nearly ruining my career."

She could only nod.

"Do you have any idea what an accusation like that does to a man, especially an innocent one? Do you?" He gave her a little shake when she didn't answer. "You could have destroyed my entire life if my department hadn't so completely believed in me."

Not so gentle now, his fingers bit into her shoulders. "You're hurting me."

With an oath he dropped his hands from her as if she'd burned him, looking as if he might be ill.

"What happened between you and Lauren?" she asked.

His laugh was cold. "The sisterly concern thing is a bit late now."

What was he saying? That everything Lauren had said was untrue? No, he hadn't actually said that, but she had to be sure. She had to know once and for all. "You and Lauren had problems," she said quietly, not wanting to ignite his temper further.

His eyes hard, expression grim, he glanced at her. "What exactly do you want to hear, Kayla? How many times I screwed around on her? Or how many times the china was broken?"

He looked angry, furious, and she stood alone with him, far from help. "Never mind," she said quickly. "I'm sorry I pried—"

"Oh, no, you're not. You're sorry you didn't find out whatever it was you wanted to know." Her fear seemed to egg him on. "Come on, Kayla, tell me the truth. You wanted to know how often I beat her, how often I gave her drugs, how often I forced her to have sex with me. Didn't you? You couldn't be bothered with her when she was alive, but now, when she's dead, you have a sudden need to hear the gruesome details."

She stared at him, wild-eyed, backing up slowly as he stalked her. At the obvious fear on her face, he exhaled sharply and stopped short.

Disgust filled his face. "I'm getting out of here now," he said in a dangerously quiet voice. "Before I prove myself the monster you think I am."

He walked away from her toward the boat.

FOUR

Kayla followed Ryan to the boat, blind to the beauty surrounding her, sure of only one thing. The man who'd helped her care for the injured duck with gentle, easy hands could never hurt her. She knew it by the way he could make Francine laugh, knew it by the look of self-recrimination on his face when she'd backed from him.

According to Lauren, Ryan had been a monster. That's what Kayla had needed to believe these past months, and now the haunting realization that she couldn't picture this man behaving that way was gut-wrenching.

What if none of it were true? What if the bruises she'd seen on Lauren were from someone else or, even worse, self-inflicted? Oh, Ryan was strong enough. She'd felt the power in him when he'd lifted her as if she weighed no more than a kitten. But she could no longer picture him hurting anyone.

Which meant she was living a lie.

It had started out nobly enough. She'd honestly believed that night, so many months ago, that she was doing the right thing. She'd been sure with every fiber of her being that a child's life unquestionably came first, even before her physician's vows. That's why when Lauren had come to her that night, hysterical and beaten to within an inch of her life, Kayla had agreed to take her infant baby—the baby no one in the family knew that Lauren had even had. The baby she'd told her husband she'd aborted when she'd been nearly four months pregnant. The baby that wasn't his.

Lindsay had so easily become Kayla's daughter.

But now that act was quite possibly based upon a lie. And Kayla hated lies. In order to live with herself, she needed to tell the truth, even if it meant exposing what she'd done in the name of love. The only thing that mattered was the truth. She had to tell it . . . and if she was right about Ryan, then he deserved to know.

Didn't he?

Ryan drove the boat in vengeful silence, and she let him. He didn't look at her, but the tension, the bitterness, the deep hurt was there for her to see in the set of his shoulders and the lines in his handsome face. The moment the boat was docked, he stalked toward the house.

She followed, unable to let it go. He knew what she'd accused him of, and yet all he'd done was react with anger—not denial or excuses, as a guilty person would have done. The implications of that hit hard as a fist to the gut.

Suddenly a thought crossed her mind—so horrible, it terrified her. What if Lauren had lied about something else? *What if she'd never had an affair?* That would make Lindsay Ryan's . . . Oh, God. Shaken, she quickened her steps in the sand to catch up to the quietly seething Ryan Scott.

Her blood roared in her ears as she stopped him at the bottom of Francine's stairs. "You said earlier that being here took you off balance," she whispered. "Why is that?"

His shoulders rose with his deep breath. "The last time I saw her was here." A harsh laugh escaped him. "She stood right in that spot you're in now and told me she'd aborted my baby."

Kayla found herself sitting on the bottom step with no recollection of getting there. "You mean right before she died?"

He gave her a funny look. "No. I never saw her again after she disappeared, all those months before that."

He'd never seen Lauren that night. Which meant he couldn't possibly have hurt her. Not questioning why she believed him, she closed her eyes and fought tears.

Kayla heard him go up the stairs, but still she didn't move.

The breath whooshed out of her. She knew Lauren had never had an abortion. She'd run away, probably hiding out with any one of her numerous wealthy acquaintances. She'd gone through with her pregnancy, for whatever reason, without fanfare. Lauren had indeed given birth. Kayla's precious Lindsay was that baby. Ryan's child. Kayla suddenly knew that without a doubt, though there'd have to be a test. But his clear eyes, wide lips, sun-kissed brown hair, even his laugh all matched Lindsay's.

Why hadn't she seen it before?

She was living a lie—a lie that was destroying Ryan's life. Yes, she'd done it in the name of love and protection and family.

But it was still a lie.

Only one thing remained, she decided as the warm winter sun glared down on her. If it turned out she'd stumbled onto the truth here, and Ryan was not only innocent of what Lauren had accused him of but was also Lindsay's father— How was she going ot make it up to him?

And how was she going to live without Lindsay?

Ryan went directly to the library, desperately in need of a diversion. He scanned the shelves for a calming book, anything to keep from contemplating strangling a particular redhead he knew.

A small leather-bound book caught his attention. Pulling it out, he stared in surprise. It was one of Lauren's diaries, probably the one Francine had mentioned. Lauren had been fanatic about them, writing daily, always locking them up afterward, taunting him with the ugly, horrifying things she'd written about him. She claimed if she died suddenly, he'd be suspected of murder.

Well, she *had* died. But the diaries had disappeared. He had no idea why this one had just turned up, and didn't care. With disgust and disinterest he shoved it back on the shelf and turned to the large set of windows.

Hadn't he suffered enough for his sins? And hadn't he tried to correct every one of them? No one had been more shocked than he when, after a month of mutually satisfying sex, Lauren had tearfully announced her pregnancy. She'd sworn she was on the pill—another lie.

Marriage hadn't been in his plans, but the idea of a child had appealed immensely. To protect that child, he'd married Lauren. But try as he might, he could never give her enough of anything—security, money, attention. She'd never been satisfied and had continued her search for happiness using sex, money, drugs . . . other men. She'd found one, too, a man, and she'd fallen in love. Or so she said. It'd been for him that she'd aborted the baby Ryan had wanted so badly.

He was still angry, he realized. And today he'd taken out that anger on the closest thing to Lauren he could get to—her sister. He could picture Kayla, talking with love about her child. Cleaning the duck's injury with the same meticulous care she would a human. Dripping wet from the dousing he'd given her. *Wet and cold*, he remembered with a physical reaction that also startled him.

He was sick, he decided. Lusting after his dead wife's sister, who had blindly believed a pack of lies about him.

He couldn't have said how long he stood there before he looked up. His heart gave a start at the sight of Kayla standing in the open door, hands braced on the doorjamb, staring at him with wide blue eyes heavy with worry and remorse. Her arms were spread, resting on the doorjamb as if she needed the support. The long, flowery dress she wore became her, hugging her willowy body, clinging to her curves. Her thick hair had been tamed into submission and pulled back from her face. As her solemn eyes met his, he had the reluctant thought—she'd never looked lovelier.

"I'm sorry," she whispered.

He couldn't take his eyes off her. "For what? Thinking the worst of me, or for wanting to believe it, even now?"

She didn't answer. "Why are you really here?" Her voice was soft and wispy, as if she were just as affected as him, and just as confused.

Was she really unaware of the danger Francine had spoken of? If so, she needed more care than he'd given. He made a promise, and he'd keep it. "Francine asked me to come." He'd been aroused from just thinking about her. Now she was there in the flesh and he ached unbearably. He didn't understand it.

"Can't you . . . go away?"

Shaking his head, he walked toward her, knowing she was about to notice the full force of his strange attraction for her. He advanced slowly, steadily, watching the color drain from her cheeks, much the way his blood had drained to the area behind his zipper.

"You—you're not thinking about Lauren."

He let out a little laugh. She had noticed. "No. Just you."

She gripped the doorjamb. "That's not wise."

He couldn't help it, he had to touch her. He fingered a strand of her silky hair. "Definitely not, no."

She swallowed hard when his fingers trailed over a cheek. She was so soft, and flushed. From his touch, he realized, studying the frantic pulse at the base of her slim throat. He felt overcome by an insane urge to press his lips to the spot.

She drew a shuddery breath. "I'm not like her."

"Thank God." His thumb slid over her jaw. "Kayla, there's something happening between us. Do you feel it?"

"I don't understand this, this—" She licked her lips, again chewed her cheek. Then abruptly changed the subject. "I'm sorry Lauren hurt you, Ryan."

His hand stilled, then lowered. "I'd rather hear you say you believe I never hurt her."

Their eyes met and held.

"I saw you at the funeral parlor," she said softly. "You were so angry. You threw things."

He could remember looking down and seeing the innocent, laughing pictures of Lauren that were to be displayed at the funeral. She'd killed their child and she still smiled sweetly. It had been too much to take and he'd gone a little crazy. "I wasn't myself. Is that when you called the cops on me?"

She closed her eyes, blushing a little. "Charges were never filed."

"Because there was no reason. And if you'd been closer to the situation, and less quick to judge, you'd have known that."

"You think I wasn't much of a sister. But I couldn't be," she whispered, pain in her voice. "Because nothing was ever enough for Lauren. I could give everything, and did for years, and it was never enough."

"I understand," he said, meaning it. He'd already forgiven her. "It was the same for me."

"Was it awful? Being married?"

"It was a match made in hell," he admitted tightly.

"What happened?"

"It started off purely physical—on both sides." He watched her shoulders tense. "She changed her mind without telling me and got pregnant. After the paternity test done through an amniocentesis, I married her. That's what she wanted."

She'd moved from him, against the window. Her dress swung gently about her body. "What did *you* want?"

"The baby," he said simply, watching a flicker of emotion light her eyes. Sympathy? he wondered. No, anguish. But why? "I didn't find out until later about her other problems."

"Drugs?" She'd stiffened again.

If only it had been that simple. "Lauren was an obsessive-compulsive, Kayla. Whatever she wanted, she wanted too much of. Money, drugs . . . men." In the end she'd been trading sex for drugs, but he spared Kayla that.

"And she told you—" She took a deep breath. "She told you that she aborted your baby?"

His stomach knotted. Over a year, and still impossible to discuss rationally. "A baby didn't suit her needs at that time. I tried to stop her." Kayla shivered, and suddenly it mattered very much what she thought of him. "Do you really think I hurt her? That I could?"

She wouldn't look at him. "You have a temper."

"Answer the question, Kayla." She turned away. He took her shoulders and gently forced her around to face him. "Oh, no, you don't, Dr. Davies. You wanted to have this conversation, and you're going to finish it. *Do you think I hurt her?*"

"I think," she said shakily, "that I'm very hungry."

He stared at her. Then the absurdity of her statement hit him and he dropped his hands from her. "What the hell does that mean?"

"Nothing. I'm just hungry. Period." She crossed her arms.

He laughed in amazement. "You *are* as loony as Lauren."

"I get hungry when I'm nervous, okay?"

"Okay," he said quietly, his amusement vanishing, hating that it was him making her nervous.

"My mother used to complain that I looked like Miss Piggy next to Lauren," she said. "But I still eat constantly."

"You could never look like Miss Piggy," he assured her. Her body was so lush and perfect, he could well imagine the envy that had inspired that statement.

Her luminous eyes met his. "I don't think you ever hurt her, Ryan. I don't think you'd hurt anyone."

He sank to the window seat, shockingly relieved. "Thank you for that," he said quietly. He pressed his thumb and forefinger hard to his eyes. "It's still a nightmare that will never end."

Overcome with guilt and a thousand other emotions she couldn't face, Kayla stepped closer. Her body came level to his face, and as he raised his head, his tortured, aching eyes drank their fill, as if he were desperate for a reprieve from the horror he had relived.

Her body tingled, and she felt vibrantly, shockingly alive.

Slowly, he stood. And when he reached for her, she didn't resist, but let him pull her into his arms, against his warm, hard chest. She could feel the sinewy strength of him, the barely restrained, almost violent passion in his taut body. It wasn't fear that made air clog her lungs, but awareness.

His eyes mirrored that awareness.

Either everything he'd just told her was the absolute truth, or he was the world's best actor. Either way, she wanted him to kiss her, and the knowledge of that was devastating.

His lips lowered, grazed hers. An electric current ran straight through her, centering between her legs. She tilted her head back for more and he gave it. With a sound low in his throat, he pulled her closer. "I'd wondered," he whispered hoarsely, drawing her earlobe between his teeth.

Her knees wobbled. "Wondered what?"

"If you liked to kiss. You have such a sexy little mouth, Kayla." His closed over hers with hunger.

Helplessly aroused, she clutched at him, then jolted sharply when the phone rang. After two more obnoxiously loud rings into the silent room, Ryan swore and snatched the phone off the hook. "Hello!"

A strange look passed over his face as he handed her the phone. "It's for you. Says he's your 'significant other.' "

She took the phone, heart still racing. "Hello?"

"Hello, gorgeous. How's things?" a deep, amused voice asked.

Matt Richardson, famous model and actor, neighbor, and, though he'd always wanted more, good friend.

Ryan, with an indecipherable look, left the room, closing the door softly behind him, leaving her with a strange sense of disappointment. "Is something wrong?" she asked Matt, giving him her attention with great effort.

"Maybe I just missed you," he teased.

" 'Significant other,' Matt? Where did that come from?"

"The guy who answered sounded . . . possessive. Someone new?"

"Ryan Scott," she said. "My sister's husband."

There was a long silence. "I thought you didn't know him."

Matt knew a mini-version of what had happened, without one major detail. He truly believed Lindsay was hers. "I don't. Didn't. Francine neglected to tell me he'd be here." And speaking of Francine, she'd been conspicuously absent. Her aunt still had questions to answer. Such as why she'd called Kayla to come in the first place. "Matt, did you need something?"

"Just . . . hurry home. We miss you, Tess, Lindsay, and I."

"I'll be there on Monday," she promised, hanging up. If he knew the half of what was happening, he'd have come for her. He was that good a friend.

He was an idiot. A fool. Ryan stalked the kitchen before dawn the next morning, unable to sleep.

Kayla had a "significant other" and he'd kissed her. He still wanted to kiss her. Just the memory had him uncomfortably hard again.

He needed out of Lake Mead, and fast.

He hadn't slept well. The insomnia didn't come from being alone—he was well used to that. Growing up in the South, it had been par for the course. Being an only child of two proud but poor Irish immigrants who'd worked day and night to provide a living had schooled him well. But he'd escaped that world long ago.

Eventually morning had dawned, and now he faced the refrigerator. And the row of various bottles of liquor on top of it. The last one was an expensive whiskey—unopened. For the first time in nearly a year he desperately wanted a drink. And then maybe another.

Frustrated, he stared at the bottle, willing the urge away. He reminded himself that he was sober today because of Francine, and all she'd ever asked for was this one favor.

The favor came through the swinging door then, wearing a long, flowing white nightgown, her beautiful hair falling past her shoulders in wild disarray. Kayla headed directly toward the goodie cabinet, but she stopped short at the sight of him.

"I didn't see you," she said in a catchy little breath, crossing her arms in front of her.

Too late, he thought. The sheer gown had afforded him a view of tantalizing, creamy, rose-tipped curves he'd never forget. He smiled as her sleepy face came wide awake. "Hungry?"

She nodded, but they both knew she lied. It was nerves that had driven her down and nothing else. She backed up until she bumped into the refrigerator. "I'm starved, actually. It's early, I know—"

He advanced as she nervously rambled, knowing he was crazy, that if he had any willpower at all, he'd get in his car and go as far as the tank would take him. But those kissable lips of hers parted as he took another step. Then she licked them. He wanted to do the same.

She was taken, and it didn't matter.

"You must be hungry too," she said quickly, jabbing a finger at him. "I'll cook up some breakfast. Maybe some eggs and—"

He took her hand and brought it to his lips, effectually cutting her off. When he kissed her palm, her eyes went cloudy with confusion and heat. Slowly, he raised her hand over her head, anchoring it against the refrigerator door, curling his other arm hard around her waist.

The only sound in the room was her uneven breathing. She closed her eyes as he nudged his hips to hers, incapable of hiding his arousal. A small sound of longing escaped her as her head thunked back against the freezer door.

Beneath the gown she was naked, and he was a goner.

"Kayla," he whispered, "I'm going to kiss you again. I have to."

She just stared at him, wide-eyed, her pulse racing.

"Don't karate-chop me to the cold tile floor, okay?"

She hesitated, then nodded.

The kiss, that first soft, gentle meeting of the lips, turned ravenous within seconds, and he drank up his fill of her sweet, warm mouth as if he were a man dying of thirst. But she was holding back, and he wanted her as out of control as he felt. He knew just how to urge her on, knew how to kiss, he'd spent most of his teenage years perfecting the technique. Within seconds he had her clutching him to her as if she couldn't stand on her own, moaning softly into his mouth and running restless hands down his body, desperate for more.

Somewhere in the dim recesses of his mind he knew it was going too far, he was allowing himself to care too much, that it had to stop—but he couldn't.

She gasped when he cupped a breast, dropping a kiss

on the silky skin that spilled out the top of her night-gown. His eyes closed in pleasure at the feel of her against his tongue, in his mouth. Holding her against the refrigerator, he wedged a knee between her thighs, thrilling to the little sound that escaped her. He was far gone, so amazingly turned on that it took him a minute to realize she was no longer kissing him back, but pushing frantically against his chest.

FIVE

With the last of her resolve, Kayla pushed at Ryan again. His slumberous eyes scanned her face, then instantly became alert.

"What's the matter?"

"I—Oh, God," she whispered, squeezing out from between him and the refrigerator. Despair nearly overwhelmed her, even as desire raged through her blood. Ryan needed to know the truth, but it was going to kill her to tell him. "This is very difficult, Ryan."

"Come on, Doc," he teased. "Kissing me couldn't have been that bad."

His light tone didn't fool her. Neither of them was breathing quite steadily, and Kayla's body was still pulsing with the strongest sense of yearning it had ever experienced. Ryan wore only a T-shirt and running shorts, both of which emphasized his powerful frame. It didn't take much to realize he was as aroused as she.

But Kayla had to be honest with him; she couldn't handle anything less than that. At this point integrity was all she had. "Ryan, we need to talk."

He immediately responded to the urgency in her

voice, the wretchedness she knew must be in her face. He touched her shoulders gently. "What is it?"

This man, the same man who had just kissed her into near oblivion, this reportedly violent and cruel man, looked directly into her eyes and waited patiently, even kindly. There was no doubt in her mind, she could no longer believe the worst of him. Which made her a far crueler person than he'd ever been reputed to be.

She'd stolen his child.

What would he do? She couldn't begin to imagine, but couldn't let that stop her. She had to be responsible for what she'd done. She had taken Lindsay with the most noble intentions. That would have to stand for something. If he pressed charges, she could go straight to jail. She'd lose her license, her right to practice, everything she'd worked for.

None of that mattered one bit to the last remaining fact—she'd lose Lindsay, her life.

She no longer had a choice. She had to tell him and risk his wrath, their growing feelings for each other, and her daughter. She had to risk everything because she could no longer live with herself if she didn't.

"Kayla?" Ryan leaned down to see her better.

"Good morning!" Francine breezed into the kitchen, dressed sportily in designer sweats. If she noticed the intensity, the proximity of her two guests, she said nothing. "My car's in town getting serviced. Ryan, would you mind driving me to get it?"

"Francine," Kayla murmured, moving away from Ryan. "We've had no time together. You disappeared on me yesterday afternoon."

"I'm sorry, darling." She smiled guilelessly. "I'll be back later. We'll talk then." She hugged Kayla close.

"I have to leave tonight," Kayla said, gripping Francine tight. The coward in her wanted to bury her face in her aunt's shoulder and never let go. "I have too much work, and—" She'd been about to say how much she missed Lindsay.

"I know. We'll talk as soon as I get back, I promise." She breezed through the door.

Ryan moved after her, glancing back at Kayla. His gaze touched on her hair, down over her body. Heat flashed between them like lightning. Unbelievably, her body responded. She had to open her mouth to breathe. His gaze lifted to her lips and lingered.

"I'll be back," he said huskily.

She laughed shakily and sank to a chair as he left, unsure as to whether he'd just made a promise or a threat.

It took Ryan several hours to get into town and back, including the brunch Francine had insisted on, and even then he returned alone. Francine had decided to stay and shop.

Ryan raced back, telling himself it was worry for Kayla that rushed him—a lie. He just wanted to see her again. Francine had again refused to discuss specifics, saying Kayla had one more day in which to tell Ryan herself. Ryan hoped Kayla hurried. Another hot kiss and he'd be unable to think, much less protect her.

The cabin was dark when he entered, though afternoon had just settled. A storm had blown in, and it was brutal. The wind was whipping up the dirt of the desert, creating a sense of isolation on the eerie, sparse land.

Kayla was nowhere to be found, though her car still remained out front.

Obviously, he thought wryly, she didn't *want* to be found. So he let her be for the moment. The heavy clouds finally let loose with the rain. The walls creaked under the strain of the wind. The windows whistled and rattled as the rain slapped against them.

Francine called from town saying she would weather the storm in the local hotel. Ryan shook his head at her overt matchmaking plan, but said nothing.

Suddenly it didn't seem like such a bad idea, him and Kayla.

The telephones went out and then the electricity. The wind howled as Ryan fumbled his way to the kitchen, intending to find a flashlight first, then Kayla. He'd left her alone long enough. He might not be able to force her to talk to him, or to accept his help, but he had to try.

He would do it because Francine had asked, but somewhere along the way it had become more than that. He'd do it because, despite the fact she was Lauren's sister, he felt inexplicably drawn to her. Remembering their searing embrace in the predawn kitchen, he grinned ridiculously, knowing she felt the same way.

As he entered the kitchen, a white-blue streak of lightning lit the room as if it were day. The refrigerator was open, and there in front of it, holding an armful of containers of food, stood Kayla clearly mortified.

It struck a chord deep within him, seeing her like that, and he could have cheerfully strangled her mother for instilling that self-consciousness in her.

The kitchen went dark again as the lightning faded. Thunder boomed. He heard the sounds of Kayla quickly shoving things back into the refrigerator, and again he felt that surge of understanding. "Do you know where the flashlights are?"

"She has none," came the quiet, embarrassed voice. "There are candles in the drawers by the stove."

Together they lit the kitchen until it glowed softly from candlelight. The flames flickered in the drafty room, sending shadows into every corner. Wearing that long, flowery dress and looking incredibly soft and beautiful, Kayla looked at him. The candles cast her in a gold glow, and he wanted to kiss her again.

Actually, he wanted more than that, wanted to sweep the candles off the table, then spread Kayla upon it, slowly opening that long row of tiny pearl buttons that fastened her dress from collar to thigh. Then he'd brush the material aside to kiss every inch of that creamy skin until she writhed beneath him.

Every ounce of blood he had drained to the pressure between his legs at the thought.

"Where's Francine?" she asked, looking desperate but not particularly hot or aching.

He sighed. So much for that fantasy. "She's staying in town tonight."

She gave him a trapped-doe look.

Move slowly, he reminded himself, lighting another candle. She's skittish, and given what he knew of her life, she was that way with damn good reason. He stopped short, then waved his fingers though the air when the match burned low enough to singe his skin. Had he just made the conscious decision that he wanted this woman in his life?

Yep.

Never one to back away from a deep thought or a confrontation, he set the match aside and moved toward her. Her brilliant blue eyes shimmered in the glowing light. Cupping her face, he slid his hands into her thick hair.

"Ryan," she said, her voice low and urgent, and he leaned closer, encouraged.

A loud crash startled them both. Ryan straightened. "What the hell was that?"

Nothing was amiss downstairs. They checked the

second floor together, by candlelight. Everything looked normal until they got to the left wing, a rarely used section with two bedrooms. Kayla opened one of the doors and immediately the source of the crash became clear.

A branch of a large tree outside had blown against the window, shattering it. Glass and water lay everywhere, over the small bed, throw rug, and . . . baby bassinet.

Shock glued Kayla to the floor and her heart squeezed painfully inside her chest. When Lauren had reappeared, she'd come to the cabin. Only after Kayla had met her there and taken the baby had Lauren driven the boat to the far east side of the lake, miles away, where the water was the deepest and roughest. She'd never come back, but this spot . . . this spot was where Lindsay had slept that night.

"Lauren bought this for the baby before she had the abortion." Ryan laughed harshly and shoved hands through his hair. "No, that's stupid, she wouldn't have bothered. Francine must have. God."

A sharp gust of wind blew in, spraying Kayla with icy rainwater, prodding her to action. She tried to close the heavy wooden shutters, but the wind was too strong and she struggled. Ryan reached around her, easily taking over.

"Careful of the glass," he said evenly, his face now carefully blank. He sat on the bed heavily, not two feet from the bassinet, staring at it with a controlled face that had Kayla's heart in her throat.

She sank down next to him. "Oh, Ryan." She had to fix this, though it would truly kill her. He'd done nothing wrong, didn't deserve the unkind twist of fate that had been dealt him because of her and her sister.

"If I had only one thing left, I'd want it to be my baby," he said in a rough whisper.

"It wasn't your fault," she told him fiercely, grabbing his forearm. "Please, Ryan, listen—"

His eyes opened. "I'd like to be alone. Please."

The starkness of his voice tore at her. She had to tell him no matter the consequences. "Ryan—"

"Go, Kayla."

"You don't understand," she said quickly. She tugged at his sleeve desperately, trying to get him to look at her. "That night, Lauren—"

"Just *go.*" His words were no more than a growl, but far more effective than a shout. "Go."

Shocked into mobility by his abrupt fury, she stood. Suddenly very unsure about being alone with him, she ran from the room, down the dark, shadowed hallway, and slammed herself into her room, locking the door behind her.

Kayla came wide awake in the middle of the night, unsure what had woken her. The rain still battered her window, the wind howled fiercely.

She'd overreacted to Ryan's anger and, remembering that, closed her eyes in shame. She'd based her reaction on what she'd spent the past year believing about him, not what she knew now.

Ryan was *not* violent or abusive, and she had nothing to fear—until she told him the truth.

In the dark night came a sound. A low moan. She flung off her covers and headed for the door, utterly incapable of ignoring the deep sound of pain.

Undecided in the dark hallway, she hesitated. When it came again, she knew. Sprinting down the hallway, she yanked open Ryan's door.

At first she couldn't see, the room was too dark and shadowed. Her eyes adjusted quickly. Ryan lay in the bed, thrashing and moaning in his sleep, deep in the throes of a violent nightmare.

"Ryan, wake up."

With a deep, heartrending cry, he tossed his arm over his eyes.

Kayla sat on the edge of his bed, her heart pounding in reaction to his horror, the fear in the sounds he made. She grasped his wide, sweat-slicked shoulders and bent over him, her heart breaking at the anguish in his face. "Ryan!" His face was tight, in a mask of deep pain, and she shook him as hard as she could. "It's a dream, just a dream. Come on, Ryan. Please, wake up."

Gasping, he gulped in a huge breath of air. Long arms snaked up, wrapping like bands of steel around her, moving suddenly to roll her beneath him, completely immobilizing her. His eyes flashed open as he flattened her with his full weight upon the bed.

"What the hell?" he rasped, blinking confused hazel eyes.

Dear God, he was completely naked. "You . . . you were having a nightmare," she said, flustered.

His eyes flashed, his arms didn't relinquish their hold, and she realized something else. He was becoming aroused. "A really bad nightmare," she added.

"Was I?" he asked softly.

She tried to act as if talking from beneath a fully aroused and naked man was an everyday occurrence, but failed miserably. "I heard you from my room."

"And you came running in here to save me from my demons." His grip tightened, and she became very aware that the only thing that separated them was her thin nightgown. "How thoughtful of you."

Casual banalities were beyond her at this point. He shifted slightly, pressing that most impressive part of him against her, and before she could stop the instinctive movement, her hips rose to meet his. He made a sound deep in his throat, lowering his mouth to her neck.

"I—" She gasped when he sucked gently at her skin. "I just wanted to make sure you were all right."

"Well, then," he murmured, working his way up to her ear. "I owe you a thank-you."

"No, really," she managed to say, sucking in her breath sharply as he tugged on her earlobe. Desire spiraled through her. "You don't."

Lightning flashed. Thunder shook the windows. Ryan lifted his head, piercing her with fully alert and awake eyes, looking rough and reckless, and dangerously, deliciously male. "I feel I must show you my gratitude."

"No, really." Was that her heart thundering in her ears? "I'll just go back to bed now and let you get some sleep."

He laughed softly and slid his hips over hers. Her heart pounded. Her blood raced. Her bones had long since melted away.

"Ryan, I—"

Her next words were lost as his mouth crashed down upon hers, matching the storm outside fury for fury.

SIX

Ryan kissed Kayla with all the urgency that drove him, haunted by the lingering memories of his nightmare and the anguish left in its midst. He felt cold to the bones. But the kiss was saving him, bringing him back from the living dead. So was having Kayla's sweet body beneath his.

He could feel her hesitation, and he sought to drive it away. Then he shivered, a remnant from his dream, he supposed, and that seemed to decide her. She made a low, concerned sound and pushed closer, lifting her head to better meet his.

The unexpected poignancy of that ripped through him, as did the way she cupped his face when his mouth devoured hers. Tenderness sprang to the surface and surprised him. He'd never felt it for a woman before, not like this. Nor had he ever been so completely aware of a woman's body. When she streaked her hands down over his bare torso, he became instantly turned on in a way that shocked him, her mere touch nearly undoing his last tiny thread of control. Then she shifted, brushing a silken thigh against him, and he nearly came right there.

She tasted as good as she smelled, and he couldn't get close enough. He tore his mouth from hers long enough to ease off her slightly, because he had to feel her, all of her, or, quite simply, he was going to die.

"Wait—Ryan, I—"

"Don't," he begged softly, kissing her when she tried to get up, moving his mouth over her eyes, her nose, the corners of her delicious mouth. "Don't say we can't, because we can." He brought the hem of her gown up her legs inch by inch, spreading his hands over her calves, then her thighs, caressing softly as he went. "Don't say it isn't right, because it is."

He heard her sharp intake of breath as his fingers brushed the very tops of her legs. "And don't say you don't want me . . ." He touched her through the thin cotton barrier. She was hot and very wet. "Because I can feel that you do." He dipped his fingers into that wetness, and she arched against him.

Grimacing as his own words and her reaction made him even harder, he brought his lips back to hers. He pushed the nightgown the rest of the way up, baring her beautiful breasts to him, and looked down at her in awe. "You're perfect," he whispered, taking a rose-tipped nipple in his mouth. She writhed against him, his name tumbling from her lips.

"What is it, sweetheart? Did I forget this one?" He brought his mouth to her other breast and laved it with equal detail as he had the first. She made a soft, sexy sound, clutching his head tightly to her.

Lightning again lit the room. When the thunder rattled the windows, she started violently in his arms. "It's all right," he murmured against her warm skin. "It's just the storm."

She didn't relax. He rose up on his elbows to smooth

back her hair, wishing for more light to see her face. "Kayla?"

"We can't," she choked out, panic in her voice. "I know you don't understand now, but we just can't. Not yet."

She trembled, and he wanted to believe it was with longing. "You want me," he said hoarsely, tasting defeat. "And I want you."

She hugged him to her, burying her face into his neck. "Please. We have to wait. I have things to tell you, things that might change how you feel about me."

Her "significant other." How conveniently he'd forgotten about him. That Kayla hadn't didn't escape him. Pushing off her, he rolled to his back, covering his eyes with a weary arm.

The only sound in the room was the wild storm and their ragged breathing that no one could mistake for anything but misplaced desire.

"I'm sorry," she whispered in the darkness.

"He must be something," he said flatly.

"He?"

"Your 'significant other,' Kayla."

She laughed weakly, shook her head. "He was just kidding, I have no one in my life like that." She sobered. "I never could have kissed you the way I did." She closed her eyes. "I got carried away. Your kisses—" Her mouth clamped shut. "I have to go."

"Go, then," he said far more harshly than he intended, driven by a deep frustration such as he'd never known. "Run away while you still can."

Listening to her race from the room, he stared blindly at the ceiling. Oh, yeah, he was in deep. Despite his best efforts to the contrary, pain and heartbreak had once again entered his life. For somehow, when he wasn't looking, Kayla had insinuated herself into his soul.

Ryan heard it at dawn, the unmistakable sound of the front door being unchained and unlocked from the inside. And he knew.

Kayla was running, escaping whatever it was between them.

He leapt from the bed and raced for the stairs, skidding at the front door, yanking it open just in time to see her car disappear down the driveway.

He shivered, realizing he stood naked in the open doorway for all the world to see. A bird scolded him and he had to shake his head.

He was a fool. But damn if he wasn't going to go after her. First of all, he still had no idea what the danger was, and he wouldn't risk her getting hurt. But also, if she felt a fraction of what he felt for her, he knew exactly how terrified she was.

Kayla took the slick roads back to Los Angeles as if the devil chased her. She told herself it was simply a reprieve from the truth she had to face.

But it was so much more than that. No longer would she simply lose her daughter, her job, her entire life.

She'd lose Ryan too.

In two short days something incredible had happened to her. To both of them. And that something would never be given a chance once she told him about Lindsay.

He'd kissed her. She'd kissed him back. Then he'd touched her and she'd gone up in flames, right there in his arms. It had taken every last ounce of resolve she had to stop him from making her feel things she couldn't afford to feel.

She'd looked up into his glowing eyes, and what she saw had startled her. She saw Lindsay's eyes, Lindsay's emotions.

Ryan was Lindsay's father. She had no doubt in her mind it was so, though there would still have to be another paternity test to prove it.

She needed to see Lindsay, hold her, and lose herself in the simple joy of her. She needed to gather all her strength and energy for what lay ahead.

One thing she knew, kids were amazingly resilient. Lindsay would come to know and love her father. She would be loved in return. No, Kayla's fear wasn't necessarily for Lindsay, it was of a more selfish nature. Ryan would remove Lindsay from her life.

Kayla had bestowed upon Lindsay all the pent-up love she had, and the baby had returned it in every hug and mushy kiss she freely gave. Knowing that their time was limited now tore at her heart. She wanted to see Lindsay again alone. Then she'd face Ryan.

Arriving home in record time, she felt exhausted. But then Tess came to the entry hall with Lindsay in her arms, both of them full of smiles. Lindsay waved her arms wildly, laughing out loud in delight at the sight of the only person she'd ever known as Mommy.

Kayla closed her eyes as she hugged the sweetest-smelling, most beautiful baby in the whole wide world, and felt her energy revitalize her. Lindsay lifted her arms and gently patted Kayla's cheeks in their own private sign for "I love you."

"Oh, Kayla," Tess murmured. "She's so sweet."

Kayla's heart cracked a little more and she hugged Lindsay so tightly, the little girl squeaked in protest.

"Hello?" a deep male voice called out.

"In here, Matt," Tess called.

He came in and kissed both Lindsay and Tess on the cheek. "Missed you," he said to Kayla with a special light in his warm brown eyes, kissing her too.

"Late night, Matt?" Tess teased. "Your car wasn't in your driveway this morning."

He looked suitably chagrined, then ruined the image by grinning wickedly. "Would you believe late night on the set?"

"No," Tess said, laughing.

Kayla managed a little smile. Matt's women were legendary.

"Hey," he said softly, dipping his head down to peer into her eyes. "You okay?"

"Just tired."

Tess and Matt exchanged a private look, then Tess reached for Lindsay. "Nap time, sweetie."

Kayla nuzzled the baby one last time and let her go.

"Want to talk about it?" Matt asked quietly when Tess had left the room with Lindsay.

Kayla sighed and moved into the living room. Standing by her large bay window, she watched the bright sun shine on her deck. How could she talk about it when she could barely face it?

"Kayla?" Matt moved to her side, watching her with concern. "Did your sister's husband do anything to upset you?"

"He's not her husband anymore, Matt."

"I see," he said quietly.

He was jealous, she realized with a pang. "It's not that," she said quickly, unwilling and unable to speak about her strange attraction to Ryan Scott. "I've just been thinking of Lauren, that's all." *And her baby.*

"Well, what did you expect, going back to that house again?" He put a friendly arm around her shoulders and hugged her. This time he let his hands linger. She tried to feel something, give back some of what she knew he felt for her. But all she could think was that they were the arms of the wrong man.

"It'd help if you put that whole thing to rest," he said quietly. "Closure, as they say."

She knew he referred to the one thing she'd never been able to do—open and sort out Lauren's safety deposit box at the bank.

Matt's eyes rested on her, full of sympathy and compassion. "I'll go with you if you want."

She'd never looked in the box, had ended up with the key only because Lauren had given it to her on that fateful night.

"Soon, Matt." She leaned into him just a little, thankful for the support.

"Okay," he murmured, squeezing her. "Let me know when. I'll be there."

Ryan glanced at the clock on the white wall in front of him. Ten A.M. Kayla had been home an hour at the most. But he could no longer delay, he had to call her. With shaking fingers he dialed.

She answered in a soft, lovely voice filled with brightness, not the wary one she used around him. Relief that she was all right came first. "Kayla? It's me."

"Ryan."

Damn her, the mistrust and vulnerability were back instantly. "I'm sorry, but you need to come back right away. It's Francine."

"What is it?"

He could feel her clutch the phone tighter, hear the insane worry that gripped her voice, and he was very sorry for it. "She fell, Kayla. Down the stairs. She's in intensive care. Drive safe." He hung up gently and turned back to the nurses' station, where the sheriff was waiting to speak with him.

Francine hadn't fallen, she'd been pushed.

Four hours later, Kayla rushed into the Nevada hospital, gaunt, tired, and ready to collapse from exhaustion. A sleepless night, two long rides through the California and Nevada desert, and now this.

Ryan stood in the middle of the waiting room, looking so familiar and surprisingly welcome that she stopped uncertainly. Solemnly, he turned to her and, without a word, opened his arms.

She let herself be drawn against his solid and warm body, feeling safe and protected, and closed her eyes to the beat of his steady heart.

"She's awake, Kayla." He still held her tight, resting his cheek on her head. "She's asking for you. After you see her, we have to talk."

Nodding, she stepped back from the securing shield of his arms. Taking a deep breath, she walked toward the nurses' station, where she was briefed on the walk to Francine's room. Multiple contusions and broken bones. Concussion. Internal bleeding.

She was a doctor, Kayla reminded herself firmly, one who saw such things daily. But nothing could have prepared her for the sight of Francine lying prone in the hospital bed, tubes and needles everywhere.

Her aunt's eyes were closed. Kayla stood looking down at the woman who'd been everything to her, mother, father, friend. Her throat closed painfully. "Oh, Frannie," she whispered.

"Kayla?" Her aunt groped for her hand. "Kayla darling . . . danger."

Kayla reached for her immediately. "I'm here, Frannie. Shhh, now." She kissed her aunt's sunken cheek and wanted to cry. "Just rest."

"Diary." Francine's head moved restlessly back and forth on her pillow, then drifted off. "Read it."

She stroked Francine's warm forehead. "Frannie?"

"Kayla's baby . . . Ryan's baby."

Kayla stilled. *"What?"* she whispered.

Francine didn't move. Kayla sagged over her, feeling as if she were losing it. Had she imagined the words? "Are you in much pain? I can get you something."

"Forgive, Kayla. You must."

"Forgive who, Frannie?" She leaned closer to catch her aunt's barely spoken words. "Tell me again."

"Forgive yourself. Love him." Francine's eyes closed again as she drifted off to a drug-induced sleep. "Love Ryan."

Love Ryan. After only two days with the man she'd once believed capable of horrible, unspeakable things, she was already more than halfway there. A nurse came in and told her Francine would sleep for hours, but she still couldn't move.

Francine lay quiet and still, a shadow of the woman she'd been. She meant everything to Kayla, everything. And she'd nearly lost her. Still could, if complications arose. One thing seemed certain: At Francine's age, she would never be the same. Kayla couldn't stop the lump from forming in her throat, or the burning behind her eyes.

"Dr. Davies?"

She lifted her head as a sheriff entered the room. "Yes?"

"I'm sorry to intrude, but I need a minute of your time."

Ryan followed him in, face and eyes grim. When she

stood, he reached for her hand. Something in the way he squeezed it had dread balling in her stomach, but she waited until they'd led her to the hallway to ask. "What is it?"

"Before your aunt lost consciousness in the ambulance," the sheriff said quietly, "she told the paramedic she didn't fall, she'd been pushed down the stairs."

Pushed. Kayla covered her mouth.

Ryan still held her hand. "Apparently she came back sometime during the night."

Their tortured gazes met.

"I didn't hear her," she whispered.

"Neither did I." Ryan's eyes held pain. "All I heard was you leaving. I ran back upstairs to . . . finish dressing. When I came back down, she'd already fallen."

"Oh, poor Frannie," she murmured, sick to her depths.

"According to the slightly jumbled statement we got, she struggled with some unknown male on the stairs," Ryan told her, once again sounding like the cop he was. "We got strands of hair and blood from beneath her fingers."

"Oh, my God," she whispered, backing to a chair. She closed her eyes for a minute, reliving the night when Lauren had come to her, beaten. She'd thought then it was Ryan. If she didn't know him now, she'd think he'd done this as well. She opened her eyes and stared directly into Ryan's dark, shuttered ones. He may have spoken coolly, professionally, but his expressive eyes couldn't hide his feelings.

He knew what she was thinking, and by the looks of him, it was killing him.

"It wasn't you," she said steadily. Nothing in his expression changed except those eyes. They filled with overwhelming relief, warm affection, and . . . something she couldn't face at the moment.

"No," he said softly, kneeling before her. "It wasn't. And for those who aren't as trusting as you, my brown hair doesn't match the light hair found on Francine."

"Then who?"

"We don't know yet, Dr. Davies," the sheriff said.

Ryan waited until the man had walked away before he wrapped his arms around her and pulled her close. "I'm sorry, Kayla, so sorry." He stood up with her, slowly rocking her back and forth in a comforting rhythm as she soaked in what had happened. She clung to him, thankful for his strength, since she had absolutely none left of her own.

"Pushed," she said in a horrified whisper. "Who broke in? Who would have pushed her, Ryan?"

"I don't know, sweetheart." He held on tight. "But we'll find out." After he checked to make sure Francine was asleep, he took her hand and led her from the hospital. She wanted to ask where they were going, but exhaustion had claimed her. Too many hours without sleep, combined with too much stress.

They didn't speak while he drove, but she felt his eyes on her often. She should have worried about work, about how they'd fill in for her for the next few days, but couldn't.

She could, she found, worry about Lindsay. She missed her baby so very much, and knew that was just the beginning.

Ryan stopped the car, but she didn't realize that they were at Francine's cabin until he pulled her out, cupped her face, and gave her a soft kiss that told her so much more than words could.

Then he took her to the boat, and she let him. For as long as she could remember, this boat had been her stress reliever. A bad grade, a fight with Lauren, her parents' indifference, a terminal patient. The completely mindless, spine-tingling speed somehow always helped. She hoped it held the magic to help one more time.

He let her drive it. She didn't speak as she pulled away from the dock, and Ryan stood silent beside her. Hitting the gas, she went full board, ignoring the wind that viciously whipped her hair about her face, the cold sting of the water that sprayed them. She lost track of time as she sped across the water, going miles and miles, zipping in and out of coves. The magnificent mountains towered over them as she got closer to the entrance of the Grand Canyon.

The weak winter sun would set any minute, and it looked so breathtaking, she felt like crying. So she did as she watched the brilliant colors streak the sky. And she knew with a bittersweetness that threatened to have her heart bursting in her chest, she would lose Lindsay and Ryan in the next few minutes. Maybe even Francine.

In all its glory, the sun moved down farther toward the canyons. Gently, Ryan pried her hands from the wheel and brought the boat to a halt, turning off the engine. He handed her a tissue. The boat bobbed on the water, not another craft or soul in sight, just high, sharp canyons surrounding them, shadows beginning to darken the water.

They were even with a large jut of rock that extended from the shore. It was flat, and just wide enough for two people to sit and watch the sun set over the immense mountains circling them. Still silent, Ryan anchored the boat, and they climbed onto the rock.

As they watched, the sun sank behind the peaks. They sat quietly as the water crashed on the rocks below, the birds chirping noisily. The air chilled.

"I shouldn't have left the hospital so abruptly," Kayla

said eventually. She sat with her arms hugging her knees, staring morosely out at the water. "There's protocol. Forms to be filled out."

"The hell with that." Ryan looked at her. "You're a distraught family member, not the rotation doctor."

The wind swirled the water, creating heavy swells. She could feel a light spray of cold water land on her skin and she turned her face into it. "Maybe Francine needs me."

In a gentler, kinder voice he said, "It'll wait, Kayla. She's resting. You should be too."

"I couldn't." She took a deep breath. "I never should have left like that. It was . . . cowardly. I hate that."

"You're not a coward. You faced me, didn't you? Even when you thought the worst. Even when you were frightened."

She knew the words cost him. "I'm sorry I hurt you, Ryan." She fell silent, knowing she would hurt him much more before it was all over.

"I never told you how much Francine means to me," he said in a low voice. "Or why."

"No," she said quietly. "I've wondered."

"My father drank." With a graceful flex of solid muscles, he threw a rock, skimming it across the water. "In spite of the old adage 'like father, like son,' I always swore to myself it could never happen to me." With a vengeance he tossed another rock. "After Lauren aborted our child, I couldn't work, eat, or sleep. I tortured myself wondering how I could have stopped her." Another rock flew. "I couldn't function."

He'd been through hell because of her family, Kayla reminded herself. She didn't deserve to comfort him.

"I started drinking," he admitted in a tight drawl. "Just like the old man that I'd sworn I'd never be like." With a sound of disgust he chucked another rock.

"Francine found out about it somehow. She lit into me, insisting I get help as loudly as I insisted I didn't need it."

"What happened?" Kayla managed to ask around the guilt that cloaked her like the winter air.

"Eventually I found a way to channel the pain and anger into something constructive. It's why I search for kids. It's not out of any big ambition to be a hotshot P.I., I just have to help somehow." He shrugged his shoulders. "And kids seem to need it most."

He looked at her then, his love and respect for Francine so evident. "She saved my life and I owe her everything for it."

She'd never met a man like him, one so honest and loyal. It was unbelievably attractive. Another light spray splashed over them, seeped into her clothes. "You said she asked you to come this weekend. Do you know why?"

He glanced away.

"Ryan."

He winced.

"It had something to do with me," she said slowly. "Didn't it?"

His jaw tightened. "Yes. She wanted me to—"

"She wanted you to—" She couldn't finish; humiliation rose and choked her. "She was playing matchmaker. Oh, my God," she whispered, dropping her head to her knees, remembering each and every kiss she'd given him, how she'd let him touch her, how he'd made her feel . . . and Francine had asked him to come. None of it had been his own idea. Heat flooded her face. "I want to go back."

She was totally unprepared for his response. He came to his knees on the wet rock and grabbed her shoulders. "Yes, dammit, Francine asked me to come.

For you. She was worried sick about something, she wouldn't say what. She wanted me to help you."

"I don't need help."

"She thinks you do. She thinks you're in danger."

"I'm not! It was a trick. A silly matchmaking trick—"

"No." His eyes, those beautiful green-brown eyes, were filled with raw pain. "It's more than that, she was so certain. She wouldn't do that, Kayla. And for the second time this year, I nearly blew something good. I nearly left, just because it was you, Lauren's sister."

"No one would have blamed you," she said flatly.

He gave her a little shake, his eyes roaming over each and every feature. "God, Kayla, don't you get it yet? I didn't stay and help just because *she* wanted me to. No one could have made me do that, not even Francine. I did it because I wanted to be with you."

Hope blossomed, to be cruelly stamped on as she remembered one thing.

Lindsay. She still had his daughter.

SEVEN

Tears misted Kayla's eyes as she stared at him, wanting so much and knowing it was all about to be taken from her. The wind screeched, the waves crashed upon the rocks.

She shivered in her damp dress, despondent and weary.

Slowly Ryan pushed to his feet, then reached a hand out to her. When she wobbled, he steadied her, smoothing back her wet hair. He murmured softly, "Kayla, we need each other. Let it be. Let it happen."

Just once, she thought, just once she deserved to live for the moment. There would be consequences, but they could be faced later.

So could the truth.

"I want you," he whispered, gliding his firm, warm lips once over hers. "So much. Want me back, Kayla."

She responded in the only way she could, tipping her face up and blindly reaching out for his mouth. What she got was the sweetest, most exquisite kiss of her life, and once they started, they couldn't stop. Desperate, aching kisses that left her so charged and needy, she could hardly stand. Ryan led her back to the boat, and she knew he would take her back to Francine's.

But that would bring reality, and reality had no place in this moment, no place at all. She wanted him now, with the glorious mountains surrounding them, the cold water spraying them, wanted him in a way she'd never wanted in her life.

In the center of the boat she walked toward him, her wet dress clinging to her legs, her unfastened hair billowing wildly. His eyes flashed as he watched her, filled with a powerful passion, a hunger, a touching amity. Her chill receded, to be replaced by an inner warmth.

He wanted her. The knowledge empowered him in a way that was new and exciting. He met her halfway with a soft, gentle kiss and warm, protective arms that glided around her without restraint. When he would have pulled away to start the boat, she stopped him.

"You don't want to go back?" he asked.

She nearly smiled at his obvious disappointment, but it was too important. And she wanted him so very much. She shook her head.

He took a deep breath, then nodded. "I understand."

"No," she whispered, tugging on his arm when he turned away again. "I don't think you do." She held on to his wonderful, sinewy arms and brought her body to a mere whisper away from his.

His eyes flared, but he didn't make it easy. "What *do* you want?"

That, at least, was simple. She threaded her hands through his thick hair and pulled his head down to hers. "Make love to me, Ryan."

His breath caught and he reached for her, pulling her hips to glide over his, telling her without words how she affected him.

"Kayla," he said in a rough, husky whisper, "here?"

She tugged him closer still and kissed him hard and deep. "Here."

His breathing was harsh, strained, and he moaned her name, kissing her back until she was too dizzy to stand. "Are you sure?" he whispered, his hands running up her spine, sinking into her hair.

No man this tender could be capable of abuse. "Yes, I'm sure."

They kneeled facing each other in the boat as the shadows deepened and the chilly air blew over them. Liquid heat shimmered through Kayla's veins. She knew she could have started a fire with her own blood. Ryan bent her back over his arm and trailed scorching kisses down her neck, making her heart leap. He traced circles on the sensitive skin beneath her breasts until she moved against him restlessly, needing more. When his thumbs skimmed over the aching, tight peaks, a jolt of desire shot straight through her.

His hands caressed their way beneath her dress and up the outside of her bare thighs. She urged him on, pressing the center of her body against his, feeling the length of him. He hissed out his breath, but his hands didn't stop their lazy ascent.

"God, Ryan. Touch me."

"I'm trying," he murmured thickly, cupping her bottom in his hands, kneading the curves, sighing in a mixture of gratification and frustration when she ground her hips to his. Fingers slipped expertly beneath the edge of her panties so that she gasped, digging her short nails into his shoulders. His fingers shifted then, and all conscious thought was swept away. She tried desperately to keep her heavy eyes open, needing to see him, but they wouldn't cooperate. Her head fell back and he nipped at her jaw, her neck, murmuring to her how good she felt, what he wanted to do to her, how she made him feel, and she could only moan, her hips rocking eagerly against his magic fingers.

"More?" he asked softly, holding her with one arm tightly around her waist as he drove her senseless. She didn't answer, *couldn't,* and he stopped.

She whimpered in bewilderment, shocked at the depth of emotion he could pull from her, at the strength of the need.

This time his voice shook slightly, sounding thick and husky. "More, Kayla?"

"Yes. God, yes," she cried.

He gave it to her, ravaging her with his mouth, his lips, his teeth. He couldn't get enough. She came in soft shudders against his fingers, and it was so remarkable, so beautiful, just watching nearly undid him. Still kneeling in the bottom of the gently rocking boat, she stared at him, her breath coming in pants, her cobalt eyes wide, her dress up past her thighs. He'd dreamed about this, just this—touching and tasting and hearing her whisper his name when he did.

"Did—did you change your mind?" she asked in a voice rough with desire, arousal.

"Never, sweetheart." Heart thundering, he reached for the buttons of her dress. To torture them both, he opened them slowly, exposing her beautiful breasts to his gaze. Closing his mouth over one, he heard her moan, felt her press closer, and lifted his head to watch her. Her hair was wildly tangled around her face, her skin flushed. Holding her gaze, he guided her hands to him, the hesitant, inexperienced way she fumbled for him making him even hotter, harder. He skimmed his fingertips over the heat of her and she was so wet, he moaned. "Kayla . . ." He tugged at her panties, and the delicate white cotton came apart in his hands. He paused, horrified, but she reached for him, struggling with his pants, giving up and cupping him through the jeans. His vision wavered.

Her breath came faster now, and at her sexy little sounds of frustration he pushed her shaking hands away and released himself. He took handfuls of her dress and shoved it up. She was whimpering with need now, so far gone she couldn't even help him. Lake water splashed over them, nearly sizzling on their hot skin, and for a second he could only stare down at her incredible body.

"Ryan." Her fingers encircled him and he went weak. He couldn't drag the air into his lungs fast enough. He wanted, needed, to lay her back and sink into her, but the bottom of the boat looked cold and wet. Then she took him and squeezed gently, pulling him toward her, and he had to be inside her. He wasn't even sure he could wait. Parting her thighs, he lifted her over him, holding her there while his eyes met hers.

"Now," she said, low and desperate, rocking against him in a motion that matched the boat's movement. "Please Ryan, now."

Obliging, he thrust up into her, swallowing her gasp of pleasure with his mouth. Wondrous. Heaven. He nearly died right there. Her muscles clamped around him as she flung her head back, her eyes tightly closed.

She was tight, so very tight, he thought, worried he'd hurt her. Control, finesse, he reminded himself, but she rubbed against his chest and then he could no longer think at all. She stretched to accommodate him as he drove himself deeper, his fingers digging into her hips as he moved. She nipped at his neck, his ear, whatever she could reach. Any semblance of control was out of the question now. Grasping her thighs, he pulled them higher, around his hips, giving him better, deeper access, and knew he'd never felt such pleasure.

More, he decided. He wanted her as desperate as he

was, wanted her to quiver helplessly around him, wanted to hear her scream for him. He sucked a puckered nipple into his mouth as he reached between their bodies where they were meshed together. She bit his shoulder, her every breath a sob. Slowly, he ran a finger over her very center, while moving within her in a rhythm as old as time. With a gasp, Kayla went still for an interminable moment in time, then cried out his name as she convulsed around him.

Watching her glorious passion, her ultimate surrender, Ryan could no longer hold back. The boat lurched over the rising swells. Water again splashed over them. None of it mattered except the woman still trembling in his arms. Ruthlessly, he drove into her again, waiting until she was spiraling helplessly before he buried his face into her neck, finally allowing himself to follow her into oblivion.

It took a herculean effort just to think clearly. Kayla knew she'd fallen limp against Ryan, and that his muscles had begun to shake, probably from supporting their weight. She shivered, and he made a sound of wordless concern, pulling her dress back together.

She looked at him, saw the guileless smile, his sparkling eyes, his lazy sense of satisfaction. And she felt like crying again.

She'd lose him.

"Ryan—"

"Shhh." His smile faded. He placed a finger to her lips, helping her rise. "Don't regret this, Kayla. Please, don't."

"It's not that." She should have told him the truth first. "I've never felt anything like it," she admitted quietly. *"Never."*

He reached for her, but she backed away. "I want to go back." She couldn't tell him about Lindsay here. Not then. Not after she'd asked him to make love to her. He'd think it had been contrived to soften him up. "Please, Ryan, take me back."

He opened his mouth, then at the fierce stubbornness on her face he shook his head and did as she asked. At her request he took her to Francine's cabin before the hospital.

She had to replace her torn underwear, still prim enough to be uncomfortable walking around without any.

Ryan didn't so much as comment as he waited at the bottom of the stairs, but she could see the wicked, knowing gleam in his eyes when she came back down. It should have embarrassed her, but somehow, with Ryan, it only made her want more.

He kissed her then, thoroughly, and she almost let it consume her again. Almost.

They drove in silence to the hospital. She wanted to check on Francine, see if the sheriff had come up with anything about Francine's break-in stranger. Ryan let her out in the lot, then grabbed her hand as she alighted from the car. "This isn't over, Kayla," he said softly, bringing her fingers to his lips.

At the sweet touch of his mouth, her eyes closed. Her heart ached.

She loved him. "It will be," she managed to say. "It will be."

Francine slipped into a coma. When Kayla, conflicted between her daughter and Francine, had to go back to Southern California the next day, Ryan was torn as well.

Nothing he could do would help Francine now, he decided, sitting by her side. Only time and luck would do that. Besides, he couldn't shake what Francine had told him about the unknown danger threatening Kayla.

Kayla believed it to be some elaborate matchmaking plan, but he wasn't so sure. Francine had seemed so positive, so worried, and he felt compelled to check it out.

Oh, hell. Who was he fooling?

He was going to go see Kayla, because already, he missed her. She wouldn't be thrilled to see him, but he couldn't stay away.

Without her he felt empty.

He'd felt that way before, plenty of times in the past year. But this time he knew how to fix it. He needed Kayla.

Still, he waited another day, staying by Francine's side in the hope she'd wake up. She didn't, but neither did her condition worsen.

He left Nevada and Lake Mead, and headed south.

Hours later, Kayla opened the door to him, wearing a sapphire-blue dress that matched her eyes, holding a little girl. When she saw him, she went perfectly still, only her eyes reflecting her joy, which was immediately replaced by a fierce inner turmoil he understood all too well.

The brown-haired toddler in her arms leveled him with a pair of laughing hazel eyes. Waving her arms, she cooed noisily, then sucked on her fingers.

He felt a pull on his heart. "Hello, Kayla." He tugged gently on a lock of Lindsay's silky hair. "Hello there, sweetheart."

Lindsay sent him a toothless smile.

Kayla didn't smile at all.

"Can I come in?"

Kayla chewed her lip, then moved aside. Her living

room was large, airy . . . and filled with toys. Pure happiness had him grinning as he looked at Lindsay. "She's beautiful, Kayla."

"You think so?"

"Yes." He wondered at the anxiety in her blue eyes. From seeing him again? She had to know he wouldn't push her, he just had to . . . Hell. He was going to push. "Kayla—"

"I'm getting Francine transferred down here so I can see her every day. She needs that."

That would be a relief for him as well. "Good. Kayla—"

"I was going to come see you tomorrow," she said, setting Lindsay down in the center of a playpen filled with soft toys. She smiled at a woman who came in and took the baby. "Thanks, Tess. She's ready for dinner."

Kayla waited until they were alone again. "I needed to talk to you about something very important."

"Is Francine okay?" he asked quickly. He'd seen her at the hospital earlier, but—

"There's no change. I hope you don't mind about me having her moved. . . ."

"No, of course not."

She took a deep breath. "What I wanted to talk to you about—"

The front door opened and a man walked in without so much as a knock. He stopped in surprise at the sight of Ryan.

"Matt?" Kayla called out. "In here."

Ryan froze. Standing there was the man who'd been Lauren's last lover. The man with whom she'd fallen madly in love. The man who'd supplied her with drugs and had manipulated her into suicide. It was for this man Lauren had aborted Ryan's child.

"Ryan, this is my neighbor—"

"Matt Richardson," Ryan said in a controlled voice. "Ryan." Matt nodded curtly.

Kayla frowned and looked at both men. Ryan's eyes had gone cold and dark, his body stiff. He looked suddenly rough and more than a little dangerous. Matt, too, had gone still, his entire body tense.

"What are you doing here?" Ryan demanded, stalking closer.

Matt's voice was slow, careful, and very deliberate. "The lady invited me."

Ryan turned disbelieving eyes to Kayla. "Tell me this isn't the 'significant other.'"

"Get out," Matt said in a territorial move that had Kayla opening her mouth to protest, but Ryan jumped in first.

"I'm here to talk to Kayla," he said through his teeth.

"Over my dead body."

"That can be arranged," Ryan said politely, shrugging out of his jacket.

"Stop it!" Kayla cried, both afraid and confused. "What's the matter with you two? How do you know each other?"

"Get out, Ryan," Matt growled. "You've done enough damage to Kayla's family, driving her sister to suicide."

With a savage snarl Ryan dove for Matt at the same instant Matt swung at Ryan. Kayla's startled scream didn't deter either one of them as they fell heavily to the floor.

"Stop it!" She bent over them just as Matt swung again and Ryan flung up an arm to block it, smacking Kayla hard in the eye with an elbow. Staggering back in surprise, she fell unceremoniously to the hardwood floor.

Both men froze, stunned, while Kayla winced and covered her aching eye. "That does it," she said much calmer than she felt. Pain arrowed through her head. "Both of you leave. *Now.*"

"Kayla." Ryan surged to his feet, then pulled her up. Regret weighed down his voice. "Let me see." He tugged on her hand covering her eye.

"No." She spun away from him, so angry she was shaking. "Leave."

"I can't," he said, trailing her. "Not until you let me see how badly you're hurt."

Furious, she walked to the front door and yanked it open. "I'll call the police, guys, trust me."

Matt moved, then paused on the threshold when Ryan remained still. Kayla didn't hesitate, refusing to be moved by those beseeching brown eyes, and she shoved Matt out hard with two hands to his chest. Turning, she stared at Ryan, who stared back. "You too."

He crossed his arms, jaw tight, eyes inscrutable. "No."

Matt still stood on the steps, waiting.

Pain radiated through her head, centering in her aching eye. Without debating her reasoning, she slammed the door on Matt and leaned her forehead against the cold wood. "I still want you to leave," she said to the door.

"I bet you do," Ryan agreed quietly, coming up behind her and turning her around to face him. "And I will, believe me. But first I want to see what I've done to you." He tipped up her head and looked into her face. His hands on her were tender, completely belying his murderous eyes.

He was furious at *her*. It was simply too much.

She shoved his hands away and tried to walk past him, but he wasn't having it. Grappling with him only further infuriated her. "That's it," she grated, trying to shake free. "Forget the explanations. Forget my eye. Just get the hell out."

"What's wrong, Kayla?" he asked in a deceptively soft voice, holding her close against him. She could feel the barely restrained violence seeping through his muscular body, the thunderous beat of his raging heart. It matched hers. "Are you frightened of the man who beat your sister and drove her to kill herself?" His grip tightened when she struggled. "Frightened I'm going to force myself on you?" Suddenly, he let her go. "Or are you just afraid—now that I've caught on?"

For an instant, panic flared as she flattened herself against the door. Somehow he'd found out about Lindsay. But that was impossible. "You didn't hurt Lauren," she whispered, sure at least about that one thing.

"Didn't I?" He grabbed her wrist in an iron grasp and dragged her into the kitchen. Thankfully, Tess and Lindsay were nowhere to be seen. He pushed her into a chair and, with surprising gentleness, pressed the ready ice pack he found in the freezer against her eye.

"Hold that," he commanded. He turned from her as if the mere sight of her sickened him. He stood at the sink, leaning on it with both arms as if he could hardly support himself. Body taut and jaw flexed, he stared out the garden window.

Rage shimmered from him, yet his eyes were filled with an anguish she didn't understand. He rolled his shoulders in a reflexive gesture that made her ache. "What's this about, Ryan?"

"You tell me."

She let out a little sound of frustration and wished things were different. "Ryan."

He paused then, came toward her in one fluid motion, moving so quickly and smoothly, she couldn't have avoided him if she'd wanted to. Grabbing the arms of her chair, he hemmed her in and leaned close. Those eyes, nearly all green with fury, speared hers. "Matt Richardson"—he nearly spat out the name—"was your sister's lover and supplier. It was he she'd convinced herself she loved, and for him that she gave up my baby."

"*Matt?*" How was that possible? She struggled to remember when exactly they'd first met. Right after Lauren died, right after Kayla had moved into this house with Lindsay. "No."

"Oh, yes, Kayla."

No . . . yet, it was possible. But if it were all true, why had Matt befriended her?

Looking grim, Ryan reached for her hand holding the ice, which she'd let fall to her lap with shock. Lifting it, he settled it with care back against her eye.

Then he turned from her and shoved his hands into his trouser pockets. "Dammit, Kayla. You knew. You had to."

"I didn't."

Ryan glanced at her, saw her watching him, and something deep within him ached. For a second, her gaze misted over with something he would have sworn was longing. His gut twisted again, because he knew the feeling. Unbidden, the memory of that night in the boat came to him. How she'd tossed her head back in wild abandon. How she'd clutched him to her in surprised joy as she'd come, almost as if she hadn't expected it.

Unbelievably, his body reacted. And with that, his anger abruptly deserted him. Her brief flare of relief when she'd first seen him that night had told him she'd missed him—whether she wanted to admit that or not.

And her sincere look of disbelieving shock at his news about Matt had been real. *It had to have been.*

"You're telling me you didn't know?" His voice sounded husky, needy, even to his own ears.

"I didn't know." She met his gaze directly. "I really didn't know."

She wasn't a liar by nature, and his instincts told him she wasn't lying then.

Which left him with one question. What the hell did Matt want with Kayla?

From somewhere on the second floor, Lindsay howled with temper. Kayla stood, set the ice on the table, revealing her quickly bruising, puffy eye. "I have to go to her."

"We're not finished. You know that."

"Yes," she said, her voice catching a little. "I know that. I still have to talk to you about something, remember?" Then she ran from the room, desperately needing to put distance between her and the man who was about to destroy her life.

EIGHT

Kayla came out of the baby's bedroom, holding Lindsay as she slurped noisily from a bottle. She stopped to hug the precious bundle to her chest. Lindsay burped indelicately, making Kayla laugh.

Then she stopped short in the hallway, her heart giving a little leap. Ryan leaned against the opposite wall, watching them, his eyes lit with an emotion she couldn't begin to name. He'd removed his tie, unbuttoned the first two buttons of his shirt, and shoved up his sleeves, making him look tough, distant, and more than a little ready for battle.

He also looked so good, her body tingled with remembrance.

"Ah . . . hi," she said stupidly. The time for the truth had come. Her smile faded. Her stomach turned over.

"Hi back." He pushed from the wall and came close in that easy-gaited, surefooted walk of his. He sent Lindsay a bittersweet smile and cupped Kayla's face with warm hands, looking at her swollen eye.

Regret crossed his features as he caressed her softly. "Does it hurt?"

What hurt was having his hands on her, knowing after she told him about Lindsay, she'd never feel them again. "Only when it's touched."

He pulled his fingers back as if she'd burned him. "God. I'm sorry."

Still drinking out of her bottle, Lindsay reached out and took a swipe at a button on Ryan's shirt. Kayla held her breath, knowing how important these moments were. Would Lindsay take to him? What would Kayla do if she didn't?

But she shouldn't have worried. Ryan held out a finger, which Lindsay promptly took in her free hand. Still slurping down her milk, she studied his hand solemnly.

Ryan's eyes seemed to beg for acceptance, and Kayla prayed that Lindsay gave it. No one moved. Then suddenly Lindsay smiled up at him, milk spilling out the corners of her mouth.

Unbearable emotion tightened Kayla's chest.

Ryan made a little face, scrunching up his mouth. Lindsay giggled, took the precious bottle from her mouth, and replaced it with Ryan's finger, slobbering all over his hand. Wonder crossed Ryan's face. Then he grinned. So did Lindsay. The two grins matched exactly, and Kayla's heart constricted even more.

She'd never needed chocolate more, Kayla thought a little desperately, turning and leading both Lindsay and Ryan out on her deck.

If she had to tell him, then she wanted it to be somewhere she felt comfortable. The deck overlooked the surrounding Angeles Crest Forest. The sun had started to set, making everything glow with gold.

It was beautiful.

The she remembered the last sunset she'd seen with

Ryan, how everything had been beautiful then too. And exactly what they'd done to add to that beauty.

Needing support for her shaking limbs, she sat at the patio table. Ryan remained standing, looking at her. She laughed nervously. "Won't you sit?"

He wanted to refuse her, she could tell by the way he set his wide shoulders, but he didn't. Impulsively, she set Lindsay in his lap. He took her effortlessly, holding on to the little squirming body with obvious pleasure. Lindsay sat facing him, playing with his buttons and occasionally tapping her open hand against his cheek in her sign of affection.

These were two of her favorite people in the entire world and they belonged together. Without her.

In the most difficult move of her life, she looked at Ryan and forced a smile, promising herself an entire gallon of ice cream for dinner. "What do you think of her?"

"She's beautiful," he said without hesitation. "You're stalling."

"Did— Did you take a good look at her?"

Ryan studied her quizzically for a minute before transferring his attention back to Lindsay. He smiled sadly into eyes that were miniature versions of his. "She reminds me of—"

"Who, Ryan?" She pushed, even as her eyes burned and her throat constricted. "She reminds you of who?"

Immense sadness and despair crossed his face. "Of what my child might have looked like if she'd been a girl. If Lauren hadn't killed her." With gentle hands that trembled slightly, he placed Lindsay back in Kayla's lap, then jerked out of his chair, striding to the edge of the deck, gripping the railing with tight hands. With his back to her he looked at the yard below.

She rose with Lindsay, coming to a stop behind him.

Nearly blind with unshed tears, she stared at his strong, taut shoulders. She hated to see him suffer, but saying it was going to destroy her.

"I think she's yours," she admitted softly.

He stiffened, then whirled to face her. "What the hell are you talking about? I didn't sleep with you until recently."

Nobody knew that better than Kayla. As a lover, he'd been masterful, sensuous, surprisingly tender, drawing emotions from her no one ever had. She'd never forget that night on the lake. Never. But this was even more important. "I know, Ryan. But it's true." Her voice broke slightly. "Lauren never had that abortion; I don't know why. She came to me claiming you weren't the father, but I think it *is* you. You have only to look at her to know it too."

His eyes lowered hungrily to Lindsay, roaming the small length of her. It hurt to see how eagerly he searched her face, hurt to know that despite her best intentions, he'd never forgive her.

"My God," he breathed, taking a step toward them. "You've had her all this time." He stopped short and lifted his hurt, shocked gaze to hers. "How long have you known?"

"I'm still not certain."

His eyes darkened. Fury settled. "Tell me, damn you."

Lindsay smiled uncertainly into Ryan's tense face, and he made the visible effort to relax.

"I started to wonder that first night at Francine's," she said quietly. "And as I got to know you, I became certain."

She knew he was rational, demonstrative, even warm-hearted. She'd seen it, experienced it herself. But now he looked mean and hard as nails.

"Let me get this straight," he said through his teeth. "You want me to believe that you didn't know about Matt and Lauren, that Lauren didn't tell you who the father of that baby was, and that you didn't see fit to tell me—her husband—that she'd had a child?"

"I—" She let go of the breath she'd been holding. She didn't have the foggiest notion of how to explain herself or to defuse his rage. "Ryan, please. Let me—"

"Give her to me," he said in a low voice. "Then leave us alone."

"I want to explain—"

"Do it."

He spoke softly, his eyes on Lindsay, obviously trying to keep her calm. Knowing it wasn't the time to point out the fact she could be wrong about Lindsay's paternity, she hugged the baby tight and kissed her, then handed her over to Ryan.

Lindsay smiled innocently at him, reaching up with a chubby hand to grab a handful of his hair against his collar. With a cherub grin she tugged hard, and he winced.

"Quite a grip," he whispered to her, his eyes bright. Lindsay laughed aloud. Looking shaky, Ryan smiled a sweet, gorgeous smile in return.

Kayla's heart fell heavily to the floor.

Turning abruptly, she ran off the deck and into the house, choked by her tears. At the glass doors she paused to look back.

Ryan hadn't moved. He stood holding Lindsay in his arms, the two of them staring at each other. Slowly, with the care of a man handling a priceless, fragile piece of china, he raised a large hand and touched her face. Lindsay smiled, and Ryan's expression softened in a way Kayla had not seen before.

In a grand gesture of camaraderie Lindsay tried to

stuff her bottle into his mouth. Ryan gave her a soft laugh that made Kayla's stomach flutter. He'd never looked so beautiful.

"Hi, baby," he said in a suspiciously wobbly voice. "I don't know what miracle brought you back to me, but I'm the most grateful daddy on this entire earth."

Ryan gently laid Lindsay in her crib. She turned herself over on her stomach, curling her legs beneath her to stick her bottom high in the air. Eyes still closed, she brought her fist to her mouth and sucked it in her sleep.

His heart overflowed just looking at her. She was the most precious thing he'd ever seen.

And she was his. He knew it now, just as he knew his own reflection. A peace he hadn't felt in two years descended over him, and for long minutes he simply stared at his perfect daughter.

Oh, he needed answers, and he'd get them. An entire year of his life had been stolen, a year he could never get back. The woman he'd let into his heart and soul had done this to him, and he wanted to know why. Reluctantly, he bent over and kissed Lindsay, stopping to inhale her sweet baby scent. She didn't budge.

Kayla had had her all along. Moving toward the door, he braced himself for a fight. He had no doubt there'd be one.

Kayla sat in her darkened living room, waiting. The evening chill had set in, but she didn't feel it, couldn't feel anything past the roar of her own blood, the heavy beat of her heart. She shivered, knowing she should light the fire. The one Tess had lit before leaving for the weekend had long since died down. But she didn't move.

And still Ryan didn't come down the stairs.

What would he do? Rant and rave? Have her arrested for kidnapping? Take Lindsay? Most certain the latter, probably the former. She jammed a fist into her mouth to stifle her cry, unable to fully accept what had happened to her perfect, sheltered little life.

A while ago, she'd called Matt, demanding explanations. He'd admitted to being hopelessly in love with Lauren, completely under her spell. He'd told Kayla that Lauren hadn't returned his love because of her fear of her husband, Ryan. Yes, Matt admitted, they did do drugs together occasionally, each supplying the other as the need arose. And when Lauren died, he'd been so desolate, so in need of comfort, he'd tried to get to know Kayla. Yet, he claimed, in the process, he'd discovered he liked Kayla even more.

Kayla didn't believe him. She felt disillusioned over the sense of betrayal, the knowledge he'd done drugs, and that he hadn't trusted her enough to tell her about Lauren.

She doubted their friendship would survive this.

Now, sitting in the living room, Kayla sucked in her breath and stilled when she finally heard Ryan's footsteps on the stairs.

"Why?" he asked hoarsely.

She closed her eyes against the pain and accusation in his voice. The knife destroying her heart twisted. "I thought I was doing the right thing."

He moved around to the front of her, a tall, vengeful figure silhouetted eerily from the light spilling from the kitchen. "Tell me, Dr. Davies, how in God's name could you have thought that? How could stealing a baby possibly have been the right thing?" His voice vibrated with tension.

"I thought you were dangerous."

His head snapped up, and though she couldn't read his expression in the shadows, she felt the stab of his stare.

"Jesus." He paced the room, his long legs churning up the open space. "You thought I was dangerous to a baby. My God."

She pushed herself to her feet and forced them to take her closer, stepping in his path, driven by the need to make him understand. "Ryan, as wrong as this sounds now, I thought I was saving her life. I had no idea you were her father. Lauren had said there was no way you could be, that you two weren't sleeping together any longer. She said if you knew she'd had an affair, you'd—"

"You convicted me, sight unseen."

She took a step backward, away from the blast of raw fury. "She said—"

"Don't," he broke in savagely. "Don't talk to me of what she told you. You *knew* she was a liar." He took a step toward her. "Tell me, Kayla. Tell me what could have possibly convinced a levelheaded, intelligent person like yourself that I was guilty without ever having set eyes on me?"

She'd expected fuming, violent rage, not this quietly furious man who was slowly backing her into a corner. "There . . . were bruises," she said unevenly. Again he advanced, and she retreated. In another minute she'd be flat against the wall. "Lauren's bruises were real, Ryan."

His face twisted. "Another Lauren tragedy, you convinced yourself. You believed her lies, even knowing how she was."

"She was terrified!" She hugged herself as she backed up. "And so was I."

He stopped abruptly, studying her thoughtfully. "You've been terrified of me this entire time?"

She hesitated, trapped.

His smile was victoriously bitter. "You were, huh? Terrified. Even when you laughed with me and tossed me to the sand at the lake? Or when we worried about Francine together?" He lowered his voice to an intimate, husky tone. "Tell me you were terrified of me that night we made love, Kayla. And I'll know you for the liar you truly are."

Her back scraped against the wall. Strong forearms flexed as he placed both hands by her head, caging her in. "Tell the truth," he said in a chilling voice. "If not to me, then at least to yourself. You knew from the minute we saw each other I would never hurt you. You knew. It wasn't me that scared you, never me. It was this damn secret."

That he was right didn't help. He stared at her as if he hated her, and it tore at her already bleeding heart. Thoughts of what might have been danced in her head, taunting, tormenting, and still her body yearned to press up against his.

As if he felt the need, too, he abruptly dropped his hands and turned away.

"I know you're hurt. And angry," she started to say.

"Don't." He dropped to the couch and slouched over, placing his elbows on his thighs and pressing his thumbs to his closed eyes. "Don't tell me how I feel, because you have no idea."

"All right, then," she said quietly. "I won't. But I can tell you how *I* felt, Ryan. Even knowing Lauren couldn't be trusted, even knowing she could stretch the truth . . . *somebody* hurt her. Badly. She really was afraid. And because of her promiscuity, I honestly believed she didn't know who the father of Lindsay was. The birth certificate has the father listed as unknown."

"Convenient." He looked at her. "Tell me every-thing, Kayla. From the beginning."

"I told you as soon as I could." She sank next to him. "It's the hardest thing I've ever done, to realize how wrong I've been."

"Dammit, you don't get it." He rose to his feet and strode to the glass doors, staring out at the dark night. "I want to hear everything that's happened to my daughter since birth. Every time she cried, every time she smiled. I want to know every little thing I've been cheated of."

"I videotaped everything," she said awkwardly, star-ing at his stiff back. "It's not enough, I know, but you can have the tapes."

"Francine knows." He laid a hand on the cold glass, trying to sort it all out. "My God, she knew and didn't tell me."

"You don't know that for certain."

No, but he'd damn well find out. He turned to take a good look at the woman who'd taken his daughter, but it was a mistake. The sight of Kayla's devastated and tear-ravaged face did something to him, something foreign, and he couldn't control the flicker of understanding or the little spear of compassion. She really had believed the worst of him, really had believed every little lie Lauren had fed her. While it didn't ease his anger, or his hurt, he found he could follow her reasoning for taking Lindsay.

But forgiveness was a long way off and forgetting was out of the question.

"I'm taking her," he said flatly. "You can have your paternity test if you want proof, but she's mine and I want her back."

Kayla stood unsteadily and nodded. Her fingers brushed over a picture of Lindsay on the table. Her eyes closed, her throat constricted, and again he felt that jerk of sympathy and unwanted understanding.

Whatever her crimes, Kayla loved Lindsay. Then a more stable emotion overcame him. *Reason.* How would he care for Lindsay? He didn't know the first thing about her. Or fatherhood. What were her needs? Could he meet them on the kind of brutal work schedule he kept?

Yes. He could and would. Whatever it took, he'd work it out.

"Get it over with," Kayla whispered into the silence.

Hearing the fear and resignation in her voice, he flipped on the lamp to see her better. "What exactly do you think I'm going to do?"

"Don't play with me, Ryan. Just do it."

"Dammit, you're the one playing games. Answer me."

She refused. Walking to the fireplace, she kneeled, reaching for paper.

Her silence only further annoyed him. "Maybe I should do as the eastern countries do—demand like for like, take something of equal value. But then, you don't have anything of equal value. Do you, Kayla?"

Striking the match with trembling fingers, she ignored him.

"Or how about the good old-fashioned American way?" he pushed, wanting a reaction. "You could be taken in for kidnapping." He caught her involuntary cringe and stared at her, stunned. "Is that what you expected me to do, have you arrested?"

Shoving the poker beneath the wood, she remained stubbornly mute.

Swearing, he lifted her up, turning her to face him. "It is, isn't it? You thought I'd throw you in jail. My

God, Kayla. You've got to stop flattering me this way, it'll go to my head."

She pushed him away. "What did you expect me to think?"

"I don't know," he said wearily. "But a little faith would have been nice. Maybe a little trust."

"I do trust you. That's why I told you."

"No," he said, shaking his head. "I was never good enough to trust. Good enough to screw, maybe, but not good enough to trust. That makes you more like your sister than you know."

"That's the second time you've compared me to her," she said, paling. "Lindsay is my life. She's my very heart, and the thought of giving her up—"

"Kills you? Yeah, I know the feeling. It happened to me."

She turned away, back to the now-crackling fire. "I thought I was doing the right thing."

He sighed. "I believe that," he told her quietly, watching her as she whirled to him in surprise. "I really do believe you thought that. But it was still wrong. No," he said harshly at the fear that filled her lovely eyes. "I'm not going to put you in jail."

"But you're taking her," she said bitterly. "So what does it matter?"

"I can't just take her," he pointed out, equally bitter. "It would terrify her to be separated from you like that. It has to be gradual."

"What are you saying?"

The hope that flared in her eyes was almost too much to take. So was the bruised swelling he'd put there. "I think I should ease into her life, over time."

"You could stay here," she said quickly, then at his raised brows she added, "On the couch. It makes into a bed. Then you won't have to disturb her sleep." She came to him, swallowing what he knew to be considerable pride and looking touchingly vulnerable. "Please, Ryan. Let's share her. For now. Until she's adjusted."

Knowing it would be the death of him to remain close to her and not be able to touch, he nodded slowly. He'd do it. For his daughter, Lindsay, he'd do anything.

In the morning Kayla tiptoed into Lindsay's room, needing a peek. But obviously she hadn't been the only one with that idea.

Wearing jeans and nothing else, Ryan stood at the crib, staring down at the sleeping baby with a look of rapt wonder on his face. Absently, he rubbed at the hard contours of his chest, as if he ached.

Again, as it had most of the night, her heart throbbed. "Good morning," she whispered, pulling her robe closer around her.

He looked deliciously rumpled, but the minute he heard her, his expression hardened.

"I'm so sorry." She forced her eyes off his bare chest, ignoring the disturbing spear of desire settling in her loins. "So very, very sorry."

He sighed and looked at her. "I'm trying very hard to believe that."

Which was more than she could ask for.

Speaking softly, he kept an eye on the baby. "I'm going to give us a couple of weeks. That should be enough time for Lindsay to get used to having me around.

"Then what?" she forced herself to ask.

"I'm not sure," he admitted. "There's a lot to consider. Tess watches Lindsay while you work?"

She nodded reluctantly. "Lindsay loves her."

"Maybe I could hire her."

"For when you take Lindsay?"

A spasm of regret crossed his face, the first sigh of softening she'd seen in him since the night before. "I'm sorry, Kayla. I'm still going to take her. She's mine."

Her stomach hurt at the finality of that statement, and she reminded herself he was mad, hurt, and feeling betrayed.

Lindsay stirred groggily, then pushed herself to a sitting position, smiling broadly at the sight of her mommy waiting. She lifted eager arms.

Hesitating, Kayla glanced at Ryan. When he nodded curtly, she scooped up the sweet, warm baby and hugged her tight. In return, Lindsay slapped two palms lightly against Kayla's cheeks, then they rubbed noses together in their morning ritual.

Ryan watched in silence, the hunger and longing showing in his expressive eyes. Wishing that those emotions were for her was useless, but at least she could try to ease his ache.

"See Ryan?" she asked Lindsay. "Want to hug him too?" She held her breath, not knowing how the typically shy Lindsay would react. But she had to try to right the wrong.

Lindsay looked at Ryan bashfully and Ryan tried not to look disappointed. Then, amazingly, Lindsay held out her arms. Ryan's face lit up as though he'd been given the world. The toughness drained, replaced by a sheer, blinding love that made Kayla's eyes sting.

Kayla stared at the wonderful man before her, yearning for things that weren't hers to have, watching as he held Lindsay close. Then he looked into Kayla's eyes; a hint of the old warmth shone brightly in his. "Thank you," he said simply.

If he kept looking at her like that, with gratitude and . . . well, not quite forgiveness, but something that at least wasn't hate, she was going to cry. "I think," she said in a trembly voice, "I'm starving."

She pushed past them both and escaped to her kitchen, where she polished off an entire box of raspberry-filled doughnuts.

Ryan buckled Lindsay into her car seat, started his car, and looked into the rearview mirror. She looked back at him expectantly.

"Hey, sweetie," he said lightly, wiping his sweaty palms on his legs. "We're off to the grocery store." He'd desperately needed out of the house, away from the woman whom he alternately wanted to strangle and then shove up against the wall to kiss senseless.

He was the one who was senseless, he decided with disgust. How could he even be thinking of Kayla that way after what she'd done to him? It made no sense.

"Mama," Lindsay gurgled in a full, pealing voice.

Ryan forced a smile, pulling out into the street. "She's waiting at home for us today. It's just you and me. Okay?"

Expecting tears, he could have soared when she smiled back. Inside the store, he got his first taste of daddyhood. Lindsay clapped in approval when he tossed ice cream in the cart. She screamed with laughter when he caught a wheel on a corner and toppled a display. And when he took out his wallet, she helped by dumping his money all over the floor.

Loading the bags back into his car, he congratulated himself on the success of the outing. He could do this, he could really do this. He could take Lindsay and they'd be fine.

But they'd be without Kayla.

Ignoring the little pang in his heart, he lifted the

chattering baby out of the cart and set her back into her car seat. She'd be a year old soon, and walking any day.

He'd missed so much and the thought only renewed his anger at Kayla. He wanted back the time he'd lost, but even as he thought that, a new set of emotions swamped him. Joy and pleasure at the second chance he'd been given with his daughter.

Kayla had given this to him, and he was grateful. As he moved around the car to get into the driver's seat, something strange happened. His cop instinct reared, and adrenaline flowed with anticipation.

Heavy footsteps came first, then the harsh breathing . . . everything that signaled danger to Ryan. Automatically, he reached for the gun that had he been on duty would have been on his hip.

Swearing, he ripped open his door and threw himself over Lindsay, just as a bullet shattered the window over his left shoulder.

Another whizzed past his ear and he tightened his death grip on the startled Lindsay, ducking his head over her and doing something he'd almost forgotten how to do.

He prayed.

NINE

"Surprised to see me?" Ryan asked Kayla through clenched teeth.

Kayla backed away from the potent fury in Ryan's eyes, away from her front door, which she'd just opened for him and Lindsay. "What are you talking about? I've been waiting and worrying for two hours. What took so long?"

Pushing past her with a sleeping Lindsay cuddled in his arms, he strode up the steps, his long legs eating them up two at a time. With amazing gentleness he laid the baby down in her crib, then whipped toward Kayla, who'd followed him. He took her arm in a grip of steel and pulled her from the room.

Resenting his use of force, Kayla tried to dig in her heels, but Ryan either didn't care or didn't notice. He tugged her down the hall, down the stairs, and into the living room, where he pushed her onto the couch. His lean form stormed around the room, and she noticed for the first time the haphazard bandage wrapped around his upper arm.

And the blood that seeped through it.

The doctor in her took over, and she rushed at him to have a look at his arm, but he wouldn't let her.

"It's just a graze." He glared at her. "A *bullet* graze." He ignored her horrified gasp and waved off her concern. "Are you going to tell me you know nothing about this?"

"Yes," she said as calmly as she could. Her insides shook. "What happened, Ryan? Is anyone else hurt?"

Coming to a restless stop at the fireplace, Ryan stood there with his head bent, staring down at the crackling fire, looking furious and discouraged. It scared her.

"Ryan."

He squeezed his eyes shut, looking like a volcano about to erupt.

She sank back to the couch. "Ryan, please."

Pushing away from the mantel, he came toward her. "Someone took potshots at us while we were in the parking lot. And we're so damn lucky not to have been killed, it's enough to make me believe in God." He hauled her up off the couch. "Now, tell me, Dr. Davies, *please.* Tell me you had nothing to do with it so I can decide if you're lying."

Rage surged through her, tainted with fear. "How dare you accuse me of such a thing!" She whirled from him, headed toward the stairs, her only coherent thought was of Lindsay.

"Wait just a minute," he grated out, yanking her back around. "You didn't answer me."

He thought she was responsible for trying to have him killed. Violent anger raced through her veins, and before she could stop herself, she swung at him. Ducking the blow as she knew he would, she moved in to toss him to the ground, but Ryan, quicker and stronger, moved first. Before she could so much as breathe, she was facedown on the carpet, securely held there by a fuming, heavy Ryan.

"Get off me," she demanded, struggling to no avail. He lay along the length of her and she could feel every contour of his hard body pressing against hers. "Let me up!" She couldn't budge him.

"You still haven't answered me," he hissed in her ear, and she was marginally satisfied to hear his quick breath, signaling that he did indeed struggle to hold her.

In the next instant he whipped her to her feet, opened the front door, and dragged Kayla outside. His car was in the driveway. The condition of it was such a shock, she would have fallen to her knees if Ryan hadn't been holding her.

Two windows had been shattered and the interior was ripped into shreds from a spray of bullets.

Tears blinded her as she thought of what could have happened to her baby, of what had happened to Ryan. "Oh my God."

"My sentiments exactly," Ryan said tersely. "The police can't believe it either."

Her vision grayed. Her world spun.

Ryan held her firmly. "If you faint now, I'll be really ticked."

Anger cleared her head immediately. But bile still rose. Shoving away from him, she ran back into the house, not wanting to make even more of a fool of herself. *Please,* she thought, *let me make it to the bathroom, where I can die in peace.*

She still had the dry-heaves when Ryan knelt beside her and handed her a damp washcloth. She closed her eyes. "Go away."

A soft sound of wordless remorse escaped him as he ran the blessedly cool cloth over her head. His gentle fingers had tears springing to her eyes again.

"Just go away."

"You didn't do it."

She wiped her mouth and sat back, curling her legs beneath her. "There's something very wrong, Ryan, that you could even think I did." She willed the nausea away and wondered how even now she could need to shove something fattening in her mouth.

"You okay?" he asked quietly.

She didn't bother to answer, but just sat there. Someone had tried to kill Ryan and Lindsay. He'd actually thought it could be her.

With amazing gentleness for a man so capable of anger, he smoothed her hair back from her face, stopping to lightly caress her still-bruised eye. His eyes met hers. "First Francine, now this. Who wants us dead, Kayla?"

They settled Francine into the local hospital that afternoon. She needed long-term care, and since she hadn't regained consciousness, it appeared she'd need it for some time to come.

Ryan insisted on helping Kayla, for which she was grateful but reserved. They hadn't exchanged another word.

Tess came along, too, and took care of Lindsay. Ryan made them come; he absolutely refused to allow Lindsay to stay home without his protection.

But it broke Kayla's heart to bring Lindsay to Francine and have Francine not even know it.

She never should have kept herself so distant from Francine for the past year. The quilt weighed heavily on her, and she wondered if and how it would all work out.

"Let it go," Ryan said quietly outside Francine's

room. Tess had taken Lindsay to be changed. "We're doing everything we can."

Kayla nodded and walked away. Ryan stared at Francine through the window of her door, lying so still. Why hadn't he pushed her for answers when she'd talked about the danger? Because he hadn't, she'd gotten hurt. Lindsay had nearly been killed.

The police had come up with nothing on the shooting and nothing on Francine's attack. Frustration welled. Moving closer to the door, he laid a hand on it and continued to look at Francine.

"Wake up, Francine," he whispered, fear in his heart. "Wake up and tell me what the hell is going on."

Her head buried in her hands, Kayla sat at her kitchen table. At the sound of Ryan's soft voice, cooing gently, she jerked her head up.

But she was all alone in the room.

"Come on, princess, you're supposed to be getting sleepy."

Relaxing, Kayla looked at the baby monitor, which she'd left on during Lindsay's afternoon nap. Ryan must be still getting his daughter ready for bed. Standing, she moved toward the counter, intending to shut the monitor off, not wanting any reminders of the man who had turned her world upside down.

"The eensy-weensy spider went up the water spout . . ."

She froze, stunned. The big, bad, dark, and angry Ryan Scott was singing to a baby.

He was singing. It shouldn't have surprised her so much, she thought, standing still in amused shock, but she couldn't easily picture Ryan as a small boy, being sung to.

Yet at that very minute, Ryan Scott was upstairs singing his very off-key heart out. Leaning against the counter, the monitor in hand, she stood there, mesmerized by the soft sound of his voice, the love that poured out in his every word to Lindsay.

"I was a very bad man today, princess," he said when the song was over. Kayla heard the rocker squeaking and knew he was holding Lindsay as he spoke. "I scared Kayla."

"Mama," Lindsay said, and the monitor spit static as she squealed with delight at her own word.

"Yes," Ryan said even more quietly. Kayla would have sworn she could hear pain in his voice. She stared at the monitor, riveted.

Ryan said, "It was very bad of me and I have to say I'm sorry to your . . . mama."

Kayla knew what that had cost him, admitting Lindsay thought of her as her mother.

"Ahhh. Gagamama," Lindsay babbled.

"You're very understanding," Ryan told her, giving her a loud kiss.

The smacking sound it made through the monitor tipped Kayla's heart on its side.

"I was angry and hurt," he told the baby. "And very afraid. Afraid for you, princess. Still doesn't excuse it though, does it?"

The rocking chair squeaked, and Kayla, frozen in the kitchen, waited as she held her breath, eavesdropping unabashedly. *He was sorry.*

"Oh," Ryan said suddenly. "Oh, boy. You need a new diaper, don't you? No wonder you won't go to sleep." He must have shifted and rose. Kayla heard the pad on the changing table as he set Lindsay down. "Now, I'm really new at this, princess. So just hold still a second—there!"

Kayla heard him open the diaper trash bag, heard the thunk as the soiled diaper hit the bottom.

"Now all we have to do is get this new one on," he told Lindsay, who cooed and babbled nonstop. Plastic rustled and the mental image of Ryan changing a diaper came to Kayla. She smiled, picturing his strong, sure hands fumbling over the job.

Then came his low, frustrated voice. "How the hell—Oh, sorry. How in the world does this thing work? This way or this way?" He muttered in a low breath. "Great. I can save you from a flying bullet and can't get a diaper on you. Some dad, huh?"

Sudden silence prevailed. Then, "Oh, jeez. Damn." More rustling, now frantic. "Princess honey, you're supposed to wait until I get a new diaper on to do that." He sighed, sounding very distressed as more rustling ensued, following by Lindsay happily chattering away.

Kayla giggled in the silent kitchen, picturing the unflappable Ryan Scott, fearless private investigator, panicking during a mere diaper change. She laughed again, then took pity as Lindsay started to fret, and she moved through the kitchen to the stairs.

Not exactly eager to see Ryan again, Kayla had given him as much space as possible all evening. In fact, she'd fully expected him to take Lindsay and leave.

He hadn't. And now, after hearing his little talk with his daughter, she thought she understood why. First, he felt badly about how'd he'd treated her, and second, he knew how attached Lindsay was to Kayla.

That he was sensitive enough to feel both those things only had Kayla hurting all the more.

In the open doorway of Lindsay's bedroom, Kayla paused. Ryan was bent over the changing table, still muttering as he struggled to clean up the mess. The room looked like a cyclone had hit it—clothes, wipes and toys strewn everywhere.

Lindsay sat smiling, completely nude, in the middle of the mess on the floor.

"Mama!" she squealed happily at the sight of Kayla.

Ryan's head whipped up and his gaze sought out hers.

Kayla bit her lip to keep her smile to herself. Ryan just stared at her, the slightest bit of warmth she'd heard him speak with only a minute before totally absent. He still wanted to be mad, she thought, understanding filling her.

And he was entitled, certainly. But he had indeed been a jerk that afternoon, and that entitled her to something of her own. The right to gloat. "What's the matter?" she asked sweetly. "Can't find her pajamas?"

He scowled.

"How's your arm?" she asked, noting he seemed pale. "Want me to take over?"

He grunted a noncommittal response.

Taking that as a firm negative, she moved into the room and scooped up Lindsay. "Hi, baby."

In silence, Ryan finished cleaning up. Kayla dressed Lindsay and set her into her crib for the night.

Lindsay immediately pulled herself upright and wailed her protest. Her father rushed to her, lifting her out.

"Ryan," Kayla chided with a shake of her head. "It's her bedtime."

"But she's crying."

Lindsay, sensing victory, clung to Ryan for all she was worth, her huge eyes drenched and hopeful.

Firmly, Kayla pried the baby from his arms and put her back into the crib. As Lindsay cried, Kayla pulled a reluctant Ryan from the room and gently shut the door.

He glared at her.

"She's taking advantage of you, Ryan. It's bedtime."

"But—" He stopped abruptly and tilted his head, listening.

Lindsay had gone silent.

He looked at her, sheepish and a little angry. "So I'm new at this. I don't have any experience, remember?"

"Yes," she said quietly. "I remember."

"I can't even get a diaper on her right." He moved past her and kept going until he stood outside on the deck, desperate for fresh air. Gripping the edge of the wood, he leaned over, letting the night air cool him off. Dammit, when would the anger go away? He'd wanted to apologize for how he'd treated Kayla earlier, and instead he'd lashed out—again.

It bugged the hell out of him that he couldn't get a grip on his emotions, that he was far too close to being the man she'd thought he was for over a year.

He needed to leave, get away from her. But he *had* to stay for Lindsay's sake. He couldn't rip his daughter from her world, not yet. If ever.

It was that last thought that terrified him.

"Officer Kent called," Kayla said softly, warily, coming up behind him. "No leads, no clues. They're calling it a drive-by shooting."

"It was deliberate." He met her hesitant eyes. "Kayla—" A disparaging sound escaped him, and he plowed his hands through his hair, wishing for peace and for the ability not to care about this woman. But it was far too late for that. "I'm sorry."

She rubbed her temples, and the sleeve of her loose blouse fell back. Sickness rose within him as he gently took her wrist.

Purplish bruises covered her fragile white skin. Bruises that he himself had put there, forcing her through the house to see his bullet-torn car. His gaze flew to hers, where he could still see the faint blue mark over her eye from the mishap of yesterday.

Kayla looked abused—and she was. By him.

Disgust welled and he turned from her, unable to face her. "I'm so damned sorry, Kayla. I never meant to hurt you."

"I never meant to hurt you either."

He took a deep breath and forced himself to look at her. "Who is, Kayla?"

Clasping her hands together, she shook her head, her eyes wide. "I don't know." Tipping her head back, rolling her shoulders as if she had kinks in them, she moved restlessly about the deck, stopping abruptly. "All I can think about, all I can see in my mind, is what happened to you and Lindsay this afternoon. And what would have happened if it'd been me instead of you."

Ryan's jaw tightened at the thought, but Kayla went on, her voice cracking. "I wouldn't have been as quick, Ryan, I know it. I would have turned in time to see her blown away before my eyes." She covered her face with her hands.

Or she herself would have been killed, he thought, struggling to remember what she'd done to him, how she'd stolen both his child and a year of his life. If he didn't continue to remember those things vividly, he would do something stupid, something he'd regret. Like hold her close and never let go.

Kayla lifted her head, her eyes bright with tears and pride. "I know you'll never forgive me. I don't know if anyone could. But I did what I did out of love for Lindsay, and I would do it again if I had to. I do love her, Ryan. More than my life."

"I know."

"And I'd get out of your life if I could, but I love her so much."

"I know that too."

"So what do we do?"

He took a deep breath and forced the calm. "We deal with this just as we are. We let Lindsay get used to me. I learn how to be a dad. And we find out what's going on."

"What's going on?" she repeated, confused.

"We find out what the danger is that Francine talked about. It's real, Kayla," he said when she paled. "It's real and I'm going to fix it."

Kayla had just added the eggs to the pan the next morning when Matt came to the back door. It was a familiar Sunday gesture, one they'd repeated often over the past year.

Kayla would cook, Matt would eat.

At his warm, hesitant smile, her mouth tightened. He'd used her, lied to her.

"Hi," he said, shoving his hands into his pockets, looking unsure of his welcome.

With good reason. She was tempted to turn her back.

She'd given it a lot of thought. Yes, Matt had known Lauren. Yes, he'd done drugs with her. And yes, he hadn't told Kayla. He'd been less than honest, but so had she. But she wasn't ready to let it go and she didn't know if she'd ever be.

"Where's our girl?" he asked, using the pet name he'd long ago given to Lindsay.

"You'd sure as hell better not be referring to my daughter," Ryan drawled, coming into the kitchen, looking lean and fit and more than a little ready to brawl in a T-shirt and snug, faded jeans.

Kayla set down her fork uneasily. This was about to get complicated.

"*Your* daughter?" Matt scowled. "No. I'm talking about Lindsay."

Okay, this was about to get more than complicated. "Matt—"

"Lindsay is my daughter," Ryan told him. "Stay away from her."

"Wait a minute." Matt moved into the room. So did Ryan.

Kayla moved between the two quickly. "Stop it. Just stop it. Ryan, I'd like to talk to Matt."

"Go ahead." He pulled out a chair, spun it around, and straddled it with his long legs, his eyes never leaving Matt.

"Oh, for God's sake," she exploded, turning off the stove and giving up on the thought of a peaceful breakfast. It wasn't going to happen, not with the raging egos battling in this room. "Matt," she said, turning her back on the infuriating Ryan, "by discussing this with you, I don't want to give you any false impressions. I'm still mad and hurt."

"I understand."

"But I haven't been completely forthright with you either," Kayla said. "And I'm sorry for that."

Matt visibly braced himself. "That's okay, Kayla. Whatever it is, it'll be okay. Just tell me," he urged.

"Lindsay is Lauren's baby. And Ryan's." There would still be a test, she and Ryan had already discussed it, but she didn't need the results to see what was right in front of her. "I've had her since the night Lauren died."

Matt gripped the table, his features slack with shock. "But I thought—"

"You thought what?" Ryan asked, his voice deceptively soft.

Matt's eyes sharpened. "You didn't know, I take it."

"Good guess. But if I had," Ryan said, still very quietly, "she never would have been allowed to get this close to you."

Was it the drugs that Lauren and Matt had shared that had made Ryan so furious at Matt, Kayla wondered, or the fact that Matt and Lauren had so obviously shared a better relationship than Lauren and Ryan had?

"You're the one who's been accused of hurting Lauren, not me," Matt stated calmly.

The air exploded with tension. Kayla could feel it emanating from Ryan's tightly coiled body. "Matt," she said quickly, "Ryan and I need to talk. You and I can finish this another time."

Matt looked down into her eyes. "I'm not sure you're safe here with him alone."

Ryan's eyes darkened dangerously.

"It doesn't matter what you think," Kayla said quickly, firmly. "I'm asking you to leave."

Matt's jaw tightened. "Kayla—"

Lindsay chose that moment to announce over the intercom that she was awake and waiting to be pampered.

"I'll go." Ryan left the room to go to his daughter without another word.

Kayla watched him, her heart aching a little at the sight of his broad shoulders squared against her. He wasn't a man to forgive and forget easily, and he still felt the pain, the bitterness of what she'd done. Of what she'd taken from him.

Soon she'd have her last day with him and Lindsay, she thought, fighting the panic. Then they'd leave her.

"Well, he's gone for the moment anyway." Matt came to her, laid his big hands on her shoulders. "I'm so sorry, please forgive me."

"Don't push me, Matt," she said with steely determination.

Matt's eyes registered surprise and hurt. "I'm not. But it's time to let go, Kayla."

"You mean just let them go? Let Lindsay go and not feel it?"

He gave her a funny look. "You said 'them.' Does that mean what I think it does?" Taking her hands in his, he frowned. "Tell me you haven't actually gotten attached to that guy."

Stubbornly, she pulled back her hands, unwilling to discuss her feelings about Ryan. She couldn't because she didn't know what they were. "This isn't about me and Ryan. This is about my life. And what it's going to be like without Lindsay in it." She sighed. "I'm sorry, Matt, I need to be alone."

"No," he said not too calmly. "Because you're not alone."

"I'll be fine," she said wearily, tired of both men.

"Kayla—" He hesitated, and that was so unlike Matt, she glanced up into his suddenly unsure brown eyes. "Now that you know how I felt about your sister, would you— Would you mind if I went through her things with you sometime?"

"You mean the security box?"

He nodded, his eyes filled with pain. "I think it would help me let go." His voice was quiet, sad. "I need to let go."

"And I need to think," she said. "Please."

He left, and she felt his disappointment keenly. But she had too many other things to think about.

Like the far too handsome man that walked back into her kitchen holding the little girl she'd loved like her own for so long. Twin sets of hazel eyes watched her.

"Keep Matt away from my daughter, Kayla," Ryan

said in an even voice that dared her to contradict him. "He contributed heavily to her mother's death, and I don't like him."

In an equally quiet voice, so as to not upset Lindsay, Kayla answered him, coming dangerously close to stabbing him with the fork she'd picked back up. "Don't talk to me of Lauren's death." She tossed the utensil in the sink, surprised at how angry she was. At herself. "Do you think I like knowing that because my sister died, I got the best year of my life?" Suddenly she felt close to tears. "That because of her death I got Lindsay? That I'd never, *ever* trade it—even if it meant giving Lauren back her life?"

Ryan found himself speechless. Slowly he set Lindsay down, struggling with how to react. He knew what he suddenly wanted to do, which was kiss her until those wide, hurting eyes were filled with hunger, but that was out of the question.

He couldn't forgive her for all she'd done. Could he?

"Oh, Ryan," Kayla cried suddenly, her face lighting up. "Look!"

Lindsay stood with one arm wrapped around the leg of the table, the other stretched out in front of her. Beaming with pride, she slowly let go of the table and staggered forward a step. Tottering for a second, she quickly took another before losing her balance and plopping down on her well-padded bottom. Beaming, she looked up at Ryan and Kayla. "Ak," she said.

"Yes," Kayla said, laughing and crouching down in front of the girl. "You walked. Oh, Mommy's so proud of you." Scooping Lindsay close, Kayla nuzzled her, then froze. She glanced up at him uncertainly, embarrassed.

Ryan kneeled down, too, so filled with pride and

love, he had to share it. He grinned at Kayla. "She's perfect, isn't she?"

She nodded, her dismayed gaze on his, and he knew why, having not missed her reference to herself as Lindsay's mommy. It was a habit, one she'd probably done a thousand times, but she now thought it wrong.

Ryan had no idea what he thought. Or maybe he did and he wasn't ready to face it. All he knew was that Lindsay was happily watching the person she thought of as her mommy, beaming with pride. Lindsay loved Kayla with all her little, giving heart. How much damage would he cause her when he took her away?

What would it do to the lovely, hurting woman at his side? And what, he wondered with sudden self-righteous anger, would it do to him to drag it out, to live like the family he'd never had and always wanted, knowing he couldn't resist her for long? He had to get away. But looking at his daughter's bright face, he had not the foggiest idea what to do.

That confusion stayed with him all day as he and Kayla sought to smooth the transition for Lindsay by hanging out together. Twice, Ryan had accidentally brushed up against Kayla, and twice his body had begged for more.

It fueled his anger and his inability to control his body's response to her. He wanted to hate her, dammit. He needed to hate her.

But he couldn't. Kayla was fascinating to watch, all graceful long limbs and beautiful, subtle movements. The hospital had called her three times, but she'd remained cool, calm, and efficient, arranging for someone else to cover for her.

He knew she couldn't stay away from work forever—neither could he. But he respected how she gave up everything to ease him into Lindsay's life.

All of which only worsened his mood.

When Lindsay went down for a nap, he headed directly toward the kitchen in search of food. Ruefully he figured he'd spent too much time with Kayla if he felt so unsettled, he needed to eat.

It shouldn't have been a surprise to find Kayla there ahead of him, rummaging through the refrigerator. She wore a soft-looking sweater, jeans, and no shoes, looking far sexier than a childnapper had a right to look. Bent at the waist, tossing things around and muttering lightly, she made quite a picture. Stepping closer, his eyes honed in on her nicely encased rear, and how it moved enticingly with her every move.

When she saw him, she let out a startled gasp, accompanied by a rain of covered containers from her hands to the floor. With a soft exclamation she stepped back and her foot landed on a plastic lid. She started to go down.

It was automatic to reach for her, but it startled them both when she ended up in his arms. He stared down at her, a little overwhelmed by how good she felt, but she pushed back, then bent to pick up what she'd dropped.

He tried to smile, but it became difficult to think, much less speak. Her sweater gaped open, giving him a peek of creamy skin and a whole host of memories of how that satiny-smooth flesh tasted and smelled. His body reacted with the predictable response. How the hell was a person supposed to stay mad, he wondered a little desperately, when his body saw things so differently from his mind?

From where she kneeled at his feet, Kayla lifted her gaze slowly, and it passed over his own jean-covered legs, then a little higher, resting at the spot where at the moment all his blood had settled. He watched her swallow hard, then further lift that gaze up past his shirt, finally to meet his eyes. Very slowly she stood, shrugging her sweater back into place, covering up those curves he remembered so well.

He wanted to touch her so badly, he shook with it.

"You ought to change that sweater," he said tightly, purposely insulting since it suited his mood to be mean. "It doesn't fit right."

"Ryan," she whispered in a voice filled with knowing regret. "Is it so hard to admit that maybe you still want me, just as you did before?"

"I *don't* want you," he said, wishing it were true. But to admit it would be to admit a whole host of other things.

Kayla looked balefully down at the distended bulge in his jeans, which blatantly proved his words a lie.

And he felt like the biggest idiot on earth. He'd fallen for Lauren, and she'd torn him to shreds. He'd just fit those pieces back together. The glue hadn't even dried yet, and here he was, about to make the same mistake again. "So I'm hard, so what?" He stepped back and just resisted the urge to cover himself up. "Your sister knew how to turn me on, why shouldn't you?"

Her mouth opened, then shut. The light went right out of her eyes, and she moved from the room, graceful and silent.

Sinking into the closest chair, he kicked a forgotten container across the room. Where was the relief? He'd finally made her good and furious.

Nope, no relief. Just the miserable feeling that he'd just made the biggest mistake of his life.

TEN

"Well, I think it was nice of him," Tess told an agitated Kayla two nights later when Kayla got home from visiting Francine.

"Nice, ha!" Kayla laughed bitterly. "Ryan isn't 'nice.' He does nothing without a purpose. He probably can't handle Lindsay alone and doesn't want to admit he needs your help."

"Kayla," her friend said gently, standing to take Kayla's hand to hold her still from her nervous pacing across the kitchen floor. "Ryan offered me the job of caring for Lindsay because you suggested it—he even said so."

Kayla sagged into a chair, the wind promptly out of her sail. "Oh." Fatigue consumed her. She'd just come off a double shift at the hospital, then had visited Francine, who had awakened. Kayla had a very long conversation with her aunt, who claimed to not remember why she'd called Kayla to the cabin nearly two weeks earlier. Worried, Kayla had called her doctor, who'd assured her Francine was improving, despite the memory lapse—which was to be expected.

Even so, Kayla had to wonder how much was a memory lapse, and how much was wise judgment, given how mad Ryan was at the prospect Francine might have known the truth about Lindsay and kept it from him.

"Have you slept at all?" Tess wanted to know.

"Some." She sighed. "I'm going to miss her so much, Tess."

"He's only at his house, Kayla, showing it to her. They'll be back later or tomorrow."

"I know. I meant I'm going to miss her when he takes her."

"He hasn't done it yet, officially. He's still staying here, isn't he?"

"Yes." Which hadn't been easy. Kayla's mouth went dry at the memory of that morning. She'd run into Ryan in the hall. He'd just walked out of the bathroom, damp from his shower, tiny drops of water glistening on his bare chest and shoulders, a towel barely hitched low at his hips. She hadn't been able to put a thought together, much less speak.

He'd given her a look when he caught her staring, a dark, dangerous, almost wicked look she wasn't likely to forget any time soon.

"Go to bed, sweetie," Tess said now. "You look like hell."

"It's only seven." Besides, she'd just lay in bed, wishing for what she couldn't have.

"Go on," Tess said, gently pushing her out of the kitchen. "I'll clean up here before I go."

Kayla went, climbing the stairs slowly. Knowing she shouldn't didn't stop her from going to Lindsay's room. Soon to be her old room.

It seemed empty without Lindsay's bright, happy face. She ran her fingers over the crib, the changing table, stared at the framed pictures on the shelves. Picking up Lindsay's favorite animal, a stuffed teddy bear, she cradled it in her arms as though she held Lindsay.

Backing to the rocker, she sank into the cushion, setting herself in motion with a small shove of her toe. Leaning back, she closed her eyes, allowing herself to pretend, just for a second, that it was Lindsay she held.

She'd done the right thing, she assured herself. She'd done the right thing.

That's where Ryan found her a half hour later.

He stood rooted, staring down at Kayla's still form as she slept in the chair. Her red hair flowed over her shoulders in waves, loose and wild. With each breath, her chest rose gently.

But it was the teddy bear that held his attention, or, rather, the desperate way she clutched it to her. It told him more about how she was feeling than she would have ever freely admitted.

Shocked at how good it was to see her after avoiding her for several days, he moved closer, a little stunned by the realization he had missed her. How could that be possible, when he was still furious about what had happened?

Absently, he rubbed his arm where the bullet had sliced his skin. Already it was healing and itchy as hell. As successful as his last two days with Lindsay had been while Kayla had worked, she'd repeatedly asked for her mother. He could have stayed at his own house with Lindsay that night, but he'd decided to bring her back. But he had to admit, Lindsay hadn't been his only reason. Tess had opened the door to them, thrilled to see Lindsay, and he'd left them downstairs in a happy reunion.

Tess warned him that Kayla had worked two very

long days at the hospital and that she was sleeping, but he'd invented some excuse to wake her up.

He'd wanted to see her. But not like this, not looking as if her best friend had deserted her. Or like her daughter had been ripped from her arms. He squatted before her, noticing the light purple rings beneath her eyes, the faint trace of tears. Her dreams weren't peaceful, he could see it in her face.

Guilt twisted his gut.

Dammit, he had a right to Lindsay; *she was his.* But Kayla was hurting and he hated that. She could have made it difficult, demanding to wait for the results of the paternity test. She hadn't, and he'd been grateful.

But he hadn't expected her to look so vulnerable, so breathtakingly beautiful. He called her name softly, wanting her to get into bed so she could sleep, as she so obviously needed to, but she didn't budge. Reaching out, he started to pull the teddy bear from her arms so he could help her up.

"No," she gasped fiercely, sitting straight up, yanking the bear back to her chest protectively. "She's mine."

"Kayla—"

"Mine, damn you."

"Kayla, it's just me. Ryan." *The asshole giving you the dreams.*

Blinking, she came instantly awake. "What are you doing here? Is something wrong with Lindsay?"

"No. I— *She* just wanted to see you."

"Where is she?"

"Downstairs with Tess."

She straightened, rubbing her eyes. The scent of her hair came to him, and he fought the craziest urge to press his face to it.

"How did the last few days go?"

"Good," he said honestly. "Great, actually."

She looked immensely relieved, which did something to his insides. Knowing she worried more about Lindsay's adjustment than her own pain humbled him to his socks.

He'd come here still angry. Thanks to her, he'd missed Lindsay's first tooth, first time to crawl, her first laugh . . . when she'd been abandoned.

The fury unexpectedly dissolved, leaving something else—admiration. She'd been there for Lindsay when he couldn't, and he should be thankful for that.

Kayla yawned, then blushed.

"Long days at work?" he asked sympathetically.

She nodded.

"Want to see her?"

Nodding again, she stood at the same time he did. They collided, a little awkwardly, and Kayla braced herself with two hands on his chest.

It was a heady feeling, having her so close, feeling her breasts brush his chest. Staring down at her, he had the strange sensation of having each sense heightened. He heard her breath catch, watched her eyes grow cloudy.

Gently he squeezed her waist as his lips lowered to hers. For one blissful minute they kissed, tormentingly sweet. Her fingers curled into his shirt, grabbing for purchase, her body melted closer to his.

Until she abruptly pulled back and raised confused eyes to his. "I thought you didn't want me," she said with torturing honesty.

He still held her. "I didn't."

"But now you do?"

He sank a hand into her glorious hair at the nape. With his other he traced a thumb over her lower lip, staring into her eyes. "Yes," he admitted softly. "I do want you."

"But you're still mad." She backed up so his hands fell to his sides.

"God, Kayla." He took a deep breath, had to just to clear his head. "I don't know. I just don't know."

"I see." She took a deep breath also, and when he reached for her again, she only shook her head. "Please, don't," she said with her usual grace and dignity, holding him off. "I really can't do this."

"Can't what?"

"Can't . . . you know."

Despite himself, he smiled at her blush. "Is it so hard to say, Kayla?"

"I can't be your lover," she said, closing her eyes as her color deepened even more. "Not with someone who likes me as little as you do." Before he could speak, she went on quickly. "I'm grateful to you, really. I appreciate you bringing Lindsay to see me, it means more than you could possibly know. But please don't kiss me anymore." She cleared her throat. "I can't resist you when you do."

She left, leaving him confused, lonely, and profoundly horny.

They lived together for the next two weeks, on and off. It wasn't easy with the tension between Ryan and Kayla, but Lindsay thrived.

So did Francine. Unfortunately, her memory did not. She still had no recollection of the weekend they'd all spent together and none of warning Ryan of any danger.

On a day Ryan got called into court on a case, Kayla—who had a rare day off—and Tess took Lindsay to the park for a picnic, not returning to Kayla's until the sun had just begun to set.

Getting out of the car, Kayla stared at her house. "Tess? I know I left the curtains shut. Did you pull that one open?"

Tess frowned at the front right window where the curtain had been shoved aside, as if someone had been looking out. "No."

Moving toward the front door, Kayla glanced up. She always left the porch light on so that if she got home after dark, she'd have some light.

It was off now.

The house felt dark and eerily silent, but Kayla saw nothing out of the ordinary. Ryan wasn't back from court. She took the sleeping Lindsay and went upstairs while Tess went to the kitchen to start some dinner.

Climbing the stairs, she squeezed the precious little girl close, knowing Ryan would come before bedtime. She'd started making herself scarce in the evenings, giving them time alone. Moving into her room, she kicked her door closed and gently set Lindsay down on the bed so she could change. She kicked off her shoes and stopped short.

Her rolltop desk was open, though she knew she'd left it shut. Someone had been in her house.

Francine had been pushed down her stairs. Then someone had shot at Lindsay and Ryan, nearly killing them both. Hastily, she grabbed Lindsay, intending to get the hell out of the house, just to be safe.

The lights flickered out before she got to the door. Terror kicked in with her pulse. With her drawn shades, specially made so that she could sleep days when she worked nights, the room was cast in pitch blackness.

Then she heard her bedroom door squeak open and she backed up, her heart in her throat. Lindsay made a small protest, and she cupped the baby's head to her chest, backing against the desk.

Something whizzed by her ear. In the dark room she heard the wood on her desk splintering as it was hit. Ducking, she dove to the left.

Smothering Lindsay close, Kayla dashed blindly toward the door. Halfway to the door, she was tripped, and she fell heavily to her side and hip, just managing to avoid falling directly on Lindsay, who whimpered in fear and confusion.

Clutching her close, Kayla scrambled to her feet. Sweat pooled at the small of her back, her breath coming in spurts she couldn't control. Cringing, she moved quickly, thinking any second her skull was going to be smashed in.

Then she realized she and Lindsay were once again alone in the room.

The light switch wouldn't work. Neither would her knees, so she sank to the floor, patting Lindsay's back uselessly.

"Kayla," came Tess's frantic voice. A beam from her flashlight flooded the room. "What were you doing in here? So much noise, you scared me to death."

Still hugging the now-sobbing Lindsay, Kayla reached for the phone by her bed. It was dead. "Didn't you see him?" she demanded, slamming down the phone.

"See who?"

The reality of what had just happened hit her, and she sagged back against the wall, trying to soothe the trembling baby. "He must have cut the phone lines and flipped the breaker—"

"Kayla," Tess gasped, sagging back against the wall as her flashlight lit her desk.

Kayla looked and what she saw chilled her to the bone. Judging from the large indentation on the desk and the hole in the wall, they were once again very lucky.

Kayla refused to think as she drove. Of course the police had nothing to go on, she thought with disgust. They'd hardly looked. In a city that continually cut their overworked staff and sliced their already dwindling budget, an attempted burglary gone awry was low priority. Her papers had been searched, yes, but no one had been hurt. She was sure there'd have been no fingerprints if they'd bothered to look.

Anger warmed her on this chilly night as the car heater had not been able to. She glanced at the sleeping Lindsay, knowing she'd sleep all the way to the cabin.

Three hours since the attack. She'd been unable to reach Ryan, had been told he was still in court. The police had been polite and patronizing, offering little help and no solutions. Unable to stay a minute longer in the house where someone had obviously been watching her, she'd headed to the one and only place she'd ever felt safe. The cabin.

Ryan wouldn't be happy to arrive and find her gone and his daughter with her. Tess was waiting at Matt's to explain, but Ryan would be panicked, furious even. He might even believe she'd run away. Maybe he'd finally have her arrested. No, she thought, that wasn't fair. Ryan wouldn't do that.

But the sheriff's car waiting in the cabin's driveway had her heart skipping a beat. With dread she faced the officer, but he explained he'd been instructed to wait for her arrival, search the inside of the cabin for intruders, and notify his commanding officer of their safety. Kayla waited warily, untrusting. But after doing just that, the officer went outside to stand guard.

Kayla knew who'd ordered the protection. And not two seconds after the front door had shut, the phone rang with a demanding, shrill sound, telling her exactly who waited impatiently on the other line.

"Hello?" she answered, palms sticky.

"Kayla." The nerves and rage in Ryan's voice was evident, and now that they were safe, she knew. *She should have waited for him, no matter her fear.*

"Hello, Ryan." The hysterical need to keep talking came from the same place her sudden insatiable hunger for cookies did. "Tess must have told you. You wouldn't have believed it," she said quickly, rambling. "He just cut the phone lines so I couldn't call out, then switched off the electricity somehow. Scared me to death, but I did know someone had been in the house because—"

"Kayla, please," Ryan cut in harshly. "Tell me you're both all right."

"We're all right. I—"

"Don't move, Kayla." The chill from his voice had goose bumps on her arms. "I'm already on my way. I'll be there in an hour—tops. We'll discuss it then."

"Ryan—" She stopped at the click and stared at the receiver. He'd hung up on her.

Tess had gotten Ryan on his cell phone and told him what happened before Ryan left the courthouse—basically, Kayla had taken off with Lindsay.

He was furious as he whipped directly from the courthouse to the cabin, but he was also afraid—an emotion that never sat well. Why had she taken Lindsay so far? To scare him? If so, she'd succeeded. Driving the narrow highway at a speed that bordered on reckless, he stared straight ahead and contemplated Kayla's slow death.

But first he wanted to see her and Lindsay and know for himself they were okay.

Alone a lot at night as a young child, Ryan had long ago learned the hard way that fear got him nowhere. Many, many nights, more than he cared to remember, he'd hear something that scared him. An old beam creak or a strange dog bark, anything. He'd panic, running into his parents' bedroom. Only he'd discover that he was alone in the house, that his parents were still at work. To his shame, he'd cry every time. How many nights had he dived into his closet, burying himself under clothes, hoping the bogeyman wouldn't find him?

Once he'd grown and put the deep South far behind him, he'd thought he'd never feel such fear again. Then Lauren had gotten ahold of him. At the prospect of losing his baby, she could terrify him more than any imagined monster ever could. Now that fear was back tenfold, and he hated the powerlessness, the helplessness of it all.

Someone was after them, he couldn't even be sure who the intended target was. First Francine, then the gunshots, now this. Who was it that was really in danger? Lindsay? Kayla? Himself?

God, he was afraid, so very afraid that he wouldn't be able to stop the next effort and protect the women he loved.

That thought so effectively froze him that he nearly killed himself on the next turn, taking it too sharply. Fighting for control on the slick Nevada desert highway, he forced a deep breath. Then shoved back his hair with a hand that shook.

Yeah, he loved her. He loved Kayla.

He slammed a fist down on the steering wheel. Impossible. Asinine. Foolhardy. Ridiculous.

All of those things, certainly. Yet it was the truth. There were only two choices. Accept it or run like hell.

Given his track record with the Davies women, he thought he should try running first.

Too bad he'd never run from a confrontation in his entire life.

ELEVEN

Ryan didn't bother to knock, but Kayla had been watching and waiting. Still, as prepared as she was, the full blast of Ryan's tangible anger staggered her. She'd anticipated the fierce expression, the stiffness of his tough body, his restlessness, but the chill in his eyes startled her.

In the face of this distant, moody Ryan, all rational thought escaped her. How to explain? How to make him understand?

"Where is she?" His voice was calm, controlled. Only the flicker of emotion in his eyes told her he wasn't calm at all.

"Sleeping."

He turned from her and took the stairs with the lithe grace of an athlete. Staring down at his daughter for a long while, he seemed to relax slightly. Gently he ran a finger over the baby's cheek. "Tell me, Kayla," he said curtly. *"All of it."*

"Here?" She knew she was stalling, but couldn't help it; she'd never seen his eyes so cold and furious.

With one last soft glance at his daughter, he walked

from the room. She again followed his tall, silent form, this time to the library. When he turned at the dark bay window and crossed his arms, giving her an impatient look, she wanted to throw something at him. Anything to break this icy calm.

"I'm waiting, Kayla."

"I told you on the telephone," she said, hating the defensive tone to her voice. Dammit, she'd been attacked! Didn't he care? "Tess, Lindsay, and I came home and someone was in the house. I went upstairs with the baby and whoever it was came at us."

"Came at you?"

His expression didn't change, and she couldn't help but wonder why he didn't seem upset for her or, at the very least, concerned.

"Well, given the size of the hole in my wall, it was probably a baseball bat." She had the satisfaction of seeing him blink in surprise and drop his arms to his sides. "My desk is ruined too." She shivered, knowing from her work experience in the emergency department exactly what kind of an impression an instrument like that could make on a skull.

Ryan studied her a moment. "The officer said that it seemed to be a strange coincidence, given the episode with the drive-by shooting."

"You talked with the police? I suppose you know, then, there's an officer outside."

"I know because I requested him." He came toward her. "Are you going to tell me what possessed you to take my daughter over two hundred miles away from me without notice? To another state even?"

She couldn't help but stare at this man she'd thought she knew. Didn't he understand what had nearly happened tonight? "You think I was trying to take her from you again."

"Were you?"

"No," she nearly shouted in frustration. "I knew you'd come. I left only because I was terrified, and in case you didn't notice, it shook me. I ran here out of impulse to keep her safe, that's it. There's no deep hidden motivation behind it, so stop looking."

"Okay," he said evenly. "I will. But until I figure out what the hell is going on, Lindsay stays away from your place."

She hated the finality to his voice, hated the authority that she herself had allowed him that gave him such a say in the first place.

"I'll find whoever is after you, Kayla."

"I hadn't realized I'd hired you."

"This isn't for you," he assured her, every bit as angry and nasty as she felt. "It's for my daughter. She loves you, and for that alone I'd do this. But the fact remains—as long as someone wants you, Lindsay's in danger as well. So promise me you'll cooperate."

"I'd never do anything to hurt Lindsay, and you know it."

He crossed the distance between them faster than she could blink. "Promise me," he said again, taking her arms in his big hands and pulling her close. "Promise me you won't ever scare me like that again."

Her breath backed in her throat as she looked into his deep hazel eyes. She saw anger, but also a helplessness she understood all too well. It was the other she hadn't been prepared to see—the genuine, soul-destroying fear.

"I promise," she said solemnly, wishing he'd free her arms so she could wrap them around him.

He did, but moved away from her quickly, crossing his arms as if he didn't quite trust himself. "I still think this may be tied in to what happened to Francine, though now she's thinking she imagined being pushed."

"What do *you* think?" she asked him. She knew Francine was confused on the details of that fateful early morning. She knew also, according to Francine, Ryan visited her daily.

"I'm not sure," he admitted, his accent twanging as it always did when he was upset. "Except it'd be very un-like her to have imagined something like that. And there's the physical evidence someone else was there." He made a face. "And now, as you know, she's claiming to forget why she called us there in the first place." He sighed the sigh of a man short of patience with the fe-male species. "But for now it's up to you to tell me everything about tonight, since Tess neither saw nor heard a thing. There's no sign of a forced entrance; in fact, there's no sign of any entrance, period."

"I didn't make it up," she said softly, shivering as she again remembered the whiz of the bat flying through the air, scantily missing her.

"Okay." He looked at her with that patient-cop look. "Tell me what you remember. I don't have much time."

"Why not?"

"I'm leaving right away. I have to be in court again tomorrow." He turned away. "And Lindsay comes with me."

Ryan and Lindsay didn't leave until nearly dawn. Kayla had told Ryan what she remembered, then Ryan had caught a few hours' sleep on the couch.

Kayla hadn't been so lucky.

But at least she didn't have to leave, since she'd worked her forty hours in two and a half days and now had two free days coming. Hurt by Ryan's assumption she'd run from him for more time with Lindsay, and bugged by the fact she couldn't seem to earn his trust, she spent the day looking in photo albums.

That proved to be depressing. Her childhood wasn't anything to remember. She'd been a plump, unhappy kid, and looking back now, she discovered the pain hadn't faded.

Running along the lake helped. So did the long, hot shower. By afternoon she felt nearly human. Except for missing Lindsay, Francine . . . and yes, dammit, Ryan.

The soothing movements of washing dishes helped dissolve her hurt and angry feelings. Why did she miss the man who continually expected her to act as her selfish, manipulating sister had? Adding more soap, she dunked a drinking glass into the hot water. Ryan had assumed the worst about her from the start. Nothing much had changed there.

She was as opposite from Lauren as anyone could get! With this vengeful thought, she applied too much force. The glass broke in two. Stunned, she stared down at her wet hand and wrist, where a bright red line of blood formed. The glass had sliced her skin in a deep cut running from palm to wrist.

Pain spread like wildfire and she sagged in defeat. Yet even now her heart hurt more than her hand. It hurt for Lindsay. For Francine too. But mostly it hurt for Ryan, who'd worked his way into her battered organ as well.

She loved the way Ryan looked at Lindsay, his eyes shining and that special smile on his face. He'd just started to look at her like that, too, before she'd told him about his daughter. Now she'd give anything to have him look at her like that again, but that wasn't going to happen.

And she had no one to blame but herself.

The blood came fast now, and with it more pain. Professionally, she studied the depth and placement of the cut, how it ran directly over the artery.

A wound like this could cause a person to bleed to death in less than an hour, she thought detachedly. If not properly treated.

It was late afternoon before Ryan learned what Lindsay was so upset about. Tess came into his living room and knew immediately, making him feel like a complete idiot.

"It's her teddy bear," she said, laughing at Ryan's look of frustration. "She doesn't like to be without it. Did you leave it at Kayla's?"

"No," he said, frustrated. "Damn."

"It's at the cabin," she said, guessing.

Lindsay started to cry again, her huge green-brown eyes filling with hot tears.

"Do you think there's something else wrong with her?" he asked Tess, feeling far out of his league. He'd had no idea how his daughter's cry could tear at his heart.

"Maybe teething."

"But you don't think so."

"No," she admitted. "I don't."

Having known Tess only a short time, he couldn't explain why he so valued her opinion. Maybe because he was desperate. "What then?"

"She misses Kayla."

"Lindsay just saw her."

"Sometimes a child just wants her mommy for no reason at all." She smiled sympathetically. "And if she can't have Mommy, she wants Teddy."

Something in Tess's tone caught his attention. "I'm not keeping Kayla from Lindsay, Tess."

He got a serious look of doubt, and silence. "I'm not," he insisted.

"She told me, Ryan."

"Told you what?" *What now?*

"What you told her last night. And it devastated her." He was leveled with a hard look. "I understand you were greatly wronged, but she feels terrible about her part in it. Lindsay and Kayla genuinely love each other. You can't keep them apart, it just isn't right."

"I have no intention of keeping them apart."

"But Kayla said you didn't want her near Lindsay anymore. I've never heard her sound so devastated. I can't imagine why she would think that—" Tess broke off as Ryan grabbed his keys. "Where are you going?"

He yanked on his jacket, muttering and swearing under his breath about the strange and alien workings of the female mind. "Can you stay with Lindsay tonight?"

"Of course."

"I'm going to the cabin to get the damned bear. Then I'm going to Kayla's to find out what the hell is wrong with that woman's hearing."

He stormed out before Tess could tell him that Kayla had never left the cabin.

On a pure whim, he went to Kayla's first, unable to get the image of her feeling devastated and depressed out of his head. *How had she possibly believed he would keep Lindsay from her?*

Hadn't he been clear?

He was forced to admit that maybe he hadn't. Had

he ever actually come out and told her she could have Lindsay whenever she wanted? No, but he'd remedy that as soon as he chewed her out for believing the worst of him.

Her car wasn't parked in front of her house, but it might have been in the garage. When she didn't answer the front door, he went to the back and knocked. No answer.

Maybe she was upstairs and couldn't hear him. Maybe she was in the shower. The thought of her there did funny things to his insides. And his outsides.

All that creamy, satiny skin . . . wet. All that wild hair . . . wet. With a groan, he forced that delicious picture away.

The back door was open, irritating him. Didn't that damn woman pay attention to his warnings? He let himself in without a thought to her sensibilities. Taking the stairs, he called out to her. No answer.

At the open door of her bedroom, he froze, sickened to the depth of his soul. He had to grab the doorjamb for support for his weakened knees.

Drywall dropped obscenely out of the gaping hole in the wall. A few feet away sat Kayla's desk, nearly broken in two from the blow it had taken. Wood had been splintered, her papers thrown in total disarray.

He'd mocked and baited her, and Kayla and Lindsay could have been killed.

She'd protected her baby with her life and he'd tormented her for running, had given her no compassion or sympathy whatsoever. He hadn't even thanked her.

Overwhelming guilt did not even come close to describing what he felt.

The long desert drive seemed to get longer each time he drove it. His short call to Tess told him what he needed to know. Kayla had never returned from the cabin.

While he berated himself over the next few hours, the mountains loomed closer, barren and cold. No less than he deserved, the icy winter air seeped through his jacket.

It was nearly ten o'clock by the time he drove up Francine's driveway. The house was dark. His entire body felt the relief at the sight of Kayla's car, but the tension didn't leave him.

What would he say to her?

The fury of what he'd discovered in her bedroom hadn't left him, though he had to control it so she wouldn't think it was directed at her. Entering, he called her name, not wanting to scare her.

A strange blue glow led him through the dark house to the kitchen.

Kayla stood in front of the refrigerator, illuminated by the little light inside the opened door. Her hair shone and that lush body, all covered up in a thick bathrobe and heavy woolen socks, was a welcoming sight. She looked like a goddess. A lovely, appealing, and very vulnerable goddess.

She looked at him without a word, without a hint of a smile he'd grown to depend on, without the slightest sign that she welcomed his presence.

His insides twisted at the thoughtless hurts he'd inflicted on this woman, the only woman who'd ever worked her way into his heart. Moving slowly, he took a step toward her, then another, until he stood directly in front of her.

Still, she said not a word as she stared at his chest, refusing to meet his eyes.

With gentle, tender hands, he cupped her face, tilting it up to his. His eyes met her stormy, defiant ones, and he felt a renewed sense of urgency to make her understand him. And forgive.

But the appropriate words to break through her armor escaped him, so he did the only thing he knew.

He kissed her.

TWELVE

Kayla tried to hold off, but in the end she gave in to Ryan's kiss because she had to, just as she had to take her next breath. He had the sexiest scent, the most wonderful feel to him, and his mouth . . . well, she was lost when he kissed her like that.

It could have been easy, with those strong arms around her, easy to forget he thought she was like Lauren, that he didn't like or trust her. Easy, but not right. She had pride, too, and right now it was screaming a warning that blasted through the haze of desire.

"No, Ryan."

He just gathered her close, bodily lifting her up against him. Again she pushed at his chest, but his arms wrapped low around her, bringing her back.

"Go home," she panted, struggling. "Go home to Lindsay."

"No," he ground out when she nearly squirmed free again. "Not until we have this out. You're upset."

"You think I'm upset?" she cried, surprisingly close to tears again, fists pounding his unrelenting shoulders. "That can't be concern I hear in your voice. You don't feel that, not for me. Only for yourself and *your* feelings, for how *you'll* be affected."

His arms still around her, Ryan backed her to the table. "I saw your bedroom, Kayla, God . . . I'm so sorry. When I think of what could have happened—" His voice broke.

"You—" Her words stopped in her throat. With the table nudging the back of her thighs, and Ryan's hips pressed to her front, there was no way to mistake his erection. "You shouldn't have come," she managed to get out.

"I had to." Effortlessly he lifted her onto the smooth surface of the wood table. In the next instant his mouth covered hers.

Her air rushed out as the wonderful, hot, swirling sensations overcame her, and the most blinding, most intense need surged. Before she could think, he'd spread her legs and moved between them to bring his hot, hard body flush to hers. His lips never left hers as those large, sure hands swept over her, and she couldn't get enough.

Pulling back only to untie her belt and yank open her robe, Ryan paused, the sight of her naked body wringing a low moan from his throat. He jerked the robe from her arms and tossed it to the tile floor, then streaked his possessive hands up her body, teasing, tormenting every inch of flesh he could reach, until she was mindless, whimpering with need.

When his fingers slid into her, she jerked against him, filled with a desperate yearning that only he could satisfy. Bending, he kissed one breast, raking the tip gently with his teeth until she writhed there on the table, surprisingly close to begging.

She reached for him, stroking him through his clothing until she felt him quiver. "Now, Ryan. Please, now."

Lifting his head, holding her stare, he spread her

thighs wider, freed himself from his jeans, and plunged into her with one sure, hard stroke. She cried out with the pure pleasure of him thick and so hard within her. He plunged deeper, burying his face in her neck and holding her tight, his breath coming every bit as harsh and raspy as hers.

The cold air blasted them from the open refrigerator, but neither noticed, using their inner heat to dispel the chill. The dark wasn't a deterrent either, for the sense of touch, smell, and taste had long since taken over.

"Lift your legs a little," he commanded in a rough whisper, spreading wet, hot, open-mouthed kisses over her heated skin, drawing shivers he instantly soothed away with questing fingers. "There, like that. Oh, God, just like that." He moaned her name as she wrapped herself around him, then thrust into her again and again, until with a helpless moan she came, splintering apart from the inside out. Within seconds he followed with his own explosive climax, pulsing powerfully within her.

They clung together, trembling with the aftermath. His cheek rested on her head and she could feel the violent thunder of his heart pounding against his ribs. Then he lifted his head, his eyes dazed, lazy, and sated. Still full of desire. Unbelievably, her body reacted again, tightening around him.

Still within her, his hips pushed against her. She could feel him hardening, which dragged another moan from her. Threading her fingers in his hair, she pistoned her hips to his.

"Kayla," he whispered, bringing his lips back to hers, gripping her waist. "Again. I want you again."

Her kiss was her response, and right there in the dark kitchen with the icy refrigerator air hitting them, she let him take her again, softer, easier, but no less soul-baringly perfect.

This time neither of them moved for long minutes.

When she could breathe, she lifted her head off his chest and stared at him, unable to believe what they'd just done. Twice.

On the kitchen table.

First in a boat. Never mind that the memory of that dark, sultry night, with the gentle rocking motion of the boat coupled with the hot rocking of Ryan's hard body, *still* made her knees weak—she still couldn't believe she'd allowed it. Now this.

Ryan looked at her questioningly, then sighed. Pulling out of her with obvious reluctance, he silently picked up her robe and handed it to her, helping her into it with surprising tenderness.

Humiliation overcame her. She'd never been into casual flings, much less making love with someone who barely liked her.

"I don't know why I let you do that," she said on an uneven breath as she pushed off the table and stood awkwardly before him, clutching her robe together and feeling ridiculously shy.

Calmly he fastened his pants. "Don't you?" he murmured.

She didn't realize she was standing there with her head bowed until he came close again, gently lifting her face.

"Kayla," he said in an achingly soft voice that unaccountably drew tears to her eyes. "I didn't come for this, but it happened. We both wanted it to. Don't regret it now."

"What did you come for?"

For a moment he didn't answer, then she shivered. A remnant from their lovemaking, or maybe just because the refrigerator door remained open, sending a draft of chilled air into the dark room.

She heard his soft oath as he moved to shut the door. It plunged them into darkness. When her eyes adjusted, she could see his outline where he stood, leaning on the refrigerator as if he needed the support.

"Lindsay needs you, she thinks you're her mother," he said so suddenly, it startled her.

"I've apologized for that," she said quietly, remorse washing over her yet again. "I don't know what else I can do—"

Moving with that lightning speed of his, he crossed the room and flipped on the overhead light. Blinking in the sudden brightness, she saw his frustration.

"She's having trouble adjusting," he told her, looking unaccustomedly helpless. "She cried a lot today."

Her heart cracked a little, picturing Lindsay crying for her. "It's a big change. It's going to take time."

His features darkened. "And that's okay with you? Just give it time and it'll work out? Meanwhile, let her cry?"

"No, it's not okay with me," she sputtered. Couldn't the man see how this killed her? "But what would you have me do? I already gave her up."

"I want you to tell me what to do, dammit."

Staring at him, the irony hit her. This big man, the one who always retained control of any given situation, wanted *her* to tell *him* what to do. She let out a little laugh.

Grasping her arms in a move that startled a gasp out of her, he pinned her to the wall so quickly, her head spun. "Laugh if you must," he spit out, "get a kick out of it. But just tell me what the hell I'm supposed to do to ease the hurt I see in my daughter's eyes."

Just as suddenly, he backed from her, his wide shoulders sagging. "You have to help me, Kayla. I can't stand the pain I've caused her."

"You didn't cause it, I did," she said wearily, wrapping her arms around herself. Experiencing the depth of feeling he had for Lindsay had her heart aching unbearably. "Oh, Ryan, I'm so sorry, so very sorry."

His eyes met hers, softening. "Just help me, Kayla. Please."

It was a struggle to remember what he truly thought of her when he looked at her like that. "You told me to stay out of her life and yours."

A frown marred that handsome face as he looked at her wrist. "I never said that."

"You did," she said with certainty. She'd never forget. "Last night. You said she had to stay away from me—"

"No." Gently he took her wrist in one large hand, turning it over to stare at the bandage she'd placed there. "I said I didn't want you to take Lindsay out alone until I found the person trying to hurt you." A spasm of pain crossed his face as he looked up at her. "You didn't really think I banished you from Lindsay, did you?" When it became evident that that's exactly what she'd thought, he swore. "I never would have done that. I told you that.

"You can see her whenever you want to," he continued in a quiet voice as he swiftly unwrapped the gauze bandage she'd placed on the nasty three-inch slice in her hand and wrist.

The generosity of his words startled her, and the tears overflowed before she could stop them. Trying to pull back her arm, she was startled when he wouldn't allow it.

His eyes had riveted to the deep, ugly cut, watching as the loosened bandage caused the blood to start flowing freely again. Swearing, he applied pressure to it and pushed her into a chair. "What the hell did you do?"

"It's nothing." She swiped at her tears with her free hand.

"It's a lot more than nothing," he said angrily. "You need stitches. Good Lord, Kayla. You're the doctor."

"Don't do this," she whispered, flinching at the pressure he applied to the cut, suddenly grateful she was sitting. "Don't act like you care. I know what you think of me."

"Do you?" he asked softly, squatting before her, using the pad of his thumb to chase away a last tear. The feel of his hand on her, even now, when she was sick with anger and remorse, did something to her. Almost against her will her cheek turned in to his hand. A strange light came into his eyes as they roamed her face, then down her body. They lingered, and though the robe was thick and more than suitably covered her, she flushed.

"All right, Doctor, if you know so much," he said, his voice thick and husky. "Suppose you tell me what I think of you."

"You . . . you think I'm like Lauren." Further words deserted her. God help her, but she couldn't possibly think with his warm hands on her, his incredible eyes looking at her like that.

Slowly, he shook his head, his expression serious. "I've said some things in anger I shouldn't have. And for that I'm very sorry. But I don't think you're like Lauren at all. I think—"

He paused when she lowered her eyes. But she couldn't stand the condemnation she knew would come. Gently he squeezed her good hand, waiting until she raised her eyes back to his. "I think you're the most loyal, sincere, and compassionate woman I've ever met."

Her breath caught.

"And a great mommy," he whispered.

She chewed her cheek and wished for a bowl of ice cream.

"Marry me, Kayla."

THIRTEEN

He'd shocked her. Hell, Ryan thought, he'd shocked himself. Sitting back on his heels, he let her absorb the marriage proposal, and took a deep breath.

No, he wouldn't take it back, not when it seemed like the perfect solution. Of course, he could have used more finesse. He *should* have used more finesse. A woman like Kayla would have to be convinced, cajoled into it.

"Why?" Kayla whispered, pulling her hands from his and wrapping them around her middle. Blood smeared onto her robe.

Alarmed, he took back her wrist, rewrapped it, then applied pressure, using the distraction to try to steady his rocked world—suddenly, it mattered very much that she say yes.

She wasn't so patient. "Why, Ryan?"

He wanted to tell her how much he loved her, but that would terrify her. Or give her a good laugh. Still holding her wrist, he stared at it. She wanted to know why, but he didn't know where to start, knew only he didn't want to be without her. "Well, there's Lindsay, of course, and—"

Standing so abruptly that her robe gaped open, Kayla shot him an unrestricted view of the most enticing breasts he'd ever had the pleasure of seeing. Jerking it shut, she ran to the door, and he didn't catch her until they were in the dark hallway.

Spinning her around, holding her, he smiled down into her stormy eyes. Unaccustomed nerves leapt in his stomach. "Didn't anyone ever tell you it's a little ungracious to walk out on a guy who's trying to propose?"

"You didn't *try*, you did it."

She looked as petrified as he felt; and his head spun as love for this woman welled up within him.

She just stared at him as if he were a madman. He felt like one. "Well?" he asked, his blood surging through his body in a raging river.

"Why?" she demanded again, her gaze unwavering. "Tell me why."

He could tell her answer was dependent on his, and he searched his mind for what she was looking for, wishing he could read hers. All he knew was that Lindsay was her biggest concern. "It's what's best for Lindsay," he said a little desperately, thinking he couldn't have come up with a more brilliant plan. For Lindsay she'd do anything, he knew it. *He hoped.*

Before his very eyes she withdrew from him. She stood right there in front of him, yet she was gone, her eyes frightfully empty.

"I can't marry you, Ryan. I'm sorry." Shrugging free, she moved past him.

The scent of her hair teased him as she went, so did the material of her robe as it clung to him. He felt so shaky watching her walk away, it was an effort to remain standing, but he wouldn't beg. "Fine," he called out tersely as she reached the top step. "Don't marry me.

But get dressed. I'm driving you to the hospital for stitches."

She faltered at the top, then shut her door without responding. It didn't matter, he'd drag her if he had to. He'd do it with pleasure.

Kayla Davies was too damned stubborn for her own good. He'd never met a more complex, vexing woman in all his life. Nor had he ever been so attracted to a woman that all his reasoning vanished just by looking into her eyes.

One look into those blue eyes tonight, and see what had happened. Right on the table they'd taken each other, rough, hard, and quick. It'd also been sensual, erotic, and the most satisfying thing he'd done in a very long time.

He wanted more, yet the door to her heart remained as tightly closed to him as her bedroom door did now.

She'd refused to marry him.

He had to have her.

Now what the hell was he going to do?

Ryan stuck to Kayla's side at the hospital, hovering protectively with an almost nervous air that would have amused her under any other circumstance. Ryan nervous was something to see. His face remained tense as the doctor checked her out, though he tried to smile at her whenever he caught her looking at him.

Obviously, he cared for her, but it wasn't enough, not for her. Not even if it meant being with Lindsay every day for the rest of her life. No, she wanted it all, and she'd settle for no less.

She wanted his love.

She flinched when the doctor injected her wound with anesthetic, then again when the needle poked and prodded deeply into the cut. Ryan squeezed her hand in sympathy, and tried to keep up the small talk, but his voice faded suddenly when the doctor held up a bigger needle.

He went white, and beads of sweat dotted his forehead.

"Ryan," Kayla suggested, amused, "sit down."

The only chair was across the room. "I'm fine," he insisted weakly. The pupils took over his gorgeous eyes. The telltale signs just about took Kayla's pain away.

She smiled, intending to tease him about being a squeamish cop, but he wavered on his feet. "Ryan?"

No response as he stared wide-eyed at her blood.

"Nurse," she said quickly and calmly, "he's going to faint."

"No, I'm not—"

But well over six feet of macho male crumpled gracefully to the floor.

"I'm not avoiding Ryan," Kayla said moodily.

"Really?" With a luxurious sigh Tess plopped down on a lounge chair on Ryan's deck. His house sat on the beach in Newport, so close they could feel the spray from the heavy waves below. She reached lazily for her iced tea. "This is the beauty of February in Southern California. Seventy-five degrees and sunny. Can't be beat." After a long sip of tea she continued. "I love Lindsay, you know I do. But it's sure nice to have a day with someone else in charge."

Kayla smiled. She was the one in charge today, and loving it. Ryan was at work and she was off and, miracle of all miracles, not on call.

According to Tess, Ryan had invited her down. He'd done that often in the past weeks, offered her Lindsay whenever she had a day off—though always through Tess. But because no leads had materialized on her assailant, Ryan still refused to let her have Lindsay at her house. Not a sacrifice, Kayla had to admit as she looked around at Ryan's gorgeous beach-front home.

But she missed living with them— *Lindsay*, she corrected herself. Not Ryan, never him. She missed the day-to-day living with her daughter.

With the monitor silent, indicating Lindsay was still napping, Kayla had time to think. Too much time.

"Are you going to tell me why you're avoiding Ryan?" Tess asked, watching her curiously.

"I'm not avoiding him." Concentrating on the huge billowing clouds lazily floating across the sky helped her look indifferent.

"You haven't seen him since that night he took you to get stitches. How come?"

"No reason." Yep, those clouds were really moving now.

"You two are crazy."

"Why?" Kayla sat up to see her friend better. "Did he say something to you?"

"No," Tess admitted with frustration. "But I've never seen two people manage to pretend not to be avoiding each other quite so well as you two."

"In case you've forgotten," Kayla pointed out dryly, "I accused him of abusing his wife, stole his child, kept her for my own, became friends with his dead wife's lover, and basically destroyed his life by not trusting him. It's no wonder he avoids me."

"You avoid him too," Tess said softly, her eyes sympathetic. "And he's gotten over most of that other stuff, I can see it. All that matters to him now is that he has Lindsay. I know something's happened. Come on, honey. Tell me."

Kayla sighed. "It's complicated."

"Complicated bad? Or complicated good?"

"He asked me to marry him."

Tess sat straight up, spilling her tea. "Wow!" She wiped up the mess and shot Kayla a thrilled look. "How positively romantic. And you said . . . ?"

"No, thank you." Restless, Kayla stood and moved to the edge of the deck, turning her face into the salty air. "Actually, I might have skipped the 'thank you' and gone directly to the 'not a chance in hell.' "

"Oh, Kayla."

"I want to marry for love, Tess."

"How do you know he wants anything less than that?"

"He just wants Lindsay happy," she said firmly.

"Look, a man who faints because you're getting stitches is a man who feels deeply for you."

"He fainted only because I was spurting blood all over him," she pointed out grimly, moving to the stairs that led down to the beach. The thought of that night and what had happened between the two of them haunted her. "Tess, I need to walk."

"Kayla—" She smiled gently when Kayla looked at her. "It'll work out if you let it."

She didn't see how it could, but she nodded. Walking along the shore with her sandals in one hand, she watched two little children run shrieking every time the water came close. Their mother laughed, running with them, scooping them close to give hugs.

Would she still be as close to Lindsay when she could run from the waves? The mother turned, and sent an open, loving smile to the man next to her. Her husband, Kayla thought with a lump in her throat as she watched the handsome man wrap an arm around the woman's shoulders. His eyes met hers, heating as the love passed between them unspoken. He pulled her close for a kiss. The children squealed.

Kayla had to look away. Would she ever see Ryan look at her like that? With love pouring from his eyes? Not in this lifetime.

Despondent, she went back to the house, entering through the kitchen.

"Ryan just got back," Tess whispered.

Just the mention of his name had her body tensing. "Bye," she whispered back, turning again to the door.

"Wait. Kayla, wait." Tess tossed down her apron and grabbed Kayla's hand. "Don't go, I just wanted you to know, that's all. I didn't want you to be startled when you saw him— Hey." She tilted up Kayla's face, inspecting it as she would have done Lindsay's if it needed to be cleaned. "You were crying."

"Was not." She moved her head, but at the stubborn look on Tess's face, sighed. "It doesn't matter. I've got to go." She ignored the inner voice that screamed "coward" and picked up her purse from the table.

"I told him you were here, Kayla."

"I can't stay," she insisted, feeling emotional. "I'm not up to it." Not up to seeing him lavish love on Lindsay, laugh with Tess, and do neither with her.

"He doesn't expect you to run off. When I told him you were here, he looked happy."

"Well, I'm not happy back. I'll just say good-bye to Lindsay real quick."

"Ryan's got her with him." Tess looked victorious. "In the shower."

"Oh, great." She plopped back into a chair and sunk her head into her hands, trying not to picture Ryan's hard body in the shower and failing hopelessly. "I can't do this," she mumbled. "I just can't."

"Can't what?" Ryan asked, coming into the room holding a happy, carefree-looking Lindsay.

That voice, Kayla thought weakly as she stood, that deep, caring voice could seduce anyone. "I can't stay," she said quickly, standing. Her purse fell, scattered, and when she bent to retrieve it, she collided with Ryan and Lindsay.

Lindsay giggled. Ryan flashed her that crooked smile that never failed to shoot straight through to her heart. "Pardon me," he drawled, effortlessly handling Lindsay as he scooped her things back into her purse. For the briefest of seconds he stilled, his eyes scanning her hospital schedule.

"You've been working too hard," he admonished her lightly.

"I'm fine," she said quickly, grabbing the purse from him and ignoring the almost electric current she felt run from his warm fingers to her cold ones. "I've got to go."

"You're not on call."

"No, but—"

"Stay, Kayla," he said softly, meeting her eyes. "We won't bite, I promise. Right, Lindsay?" He tickled the baby under her chin, evoking peals of laughter.

Kayla could only stare at her previously shy and quiet baby. "You've done wonders for her, Ryan. She looks so happy."

"She misses you," he said, his smile fading a little. He put Lindsay into her arms, and for an endless minute their limbs brushed together, creating a sense of delicious friction. Kayla closed her eyes against it, but it only got stronger.

When she looked at him again, he'd moved even closer, his eyes shining with warmth and affection as he watched the baby throw her arms around Kayla's neck. "Stay for dinner."

His hair lay wet and curled against his collar. The scent of his soap came to her, as did the scent of the man. It would be too much to resist, she thought, especially since she'd so easily convinced herself that Ryan's show of emotion had been for her.

It hadn't. It couldn't. It had been for Lindsay.

"I—" she started to say, but he covered her mouth with his fingers.

"Please," he whispered. "If not for me, then for Lindsay."

In the awkward silence that followed, while Kayla fought for air and control, Tess came forward and took Lindsay. With a sly glance at Kayla she moved from the room, saying she was going to change the baby.

Ryan's knowing smile said he didn't mind Tess's overt move to get them alone.

Kayla longingly glanced at the wooden bread box, which held a box of doughnuts.

Ryan laughed softly. "Hungry?" he asked, tugging on a lock of hair until she looked at him. "Or just nervous?"

She bit her cheek and narrowed her eyes on him. "Hungry, of course. You don't make me nervous."

He let that go, lifted her hand, and kissed her fingers.

Her breath stopped. At her betraying tremor, he smiled and kissed her palm. "I have ice cream," he murmured, working his way up her wrist with his incredibly talented tongue. "If you just admit it's me making you tremble, you can have the entire gallon."

She tried to yank her hand back, but he held tight, regretfully studying the small bandage on her wrist. "You're okay?"

"Yes, thanks to you."

"Oh, yeah." His voice was sarcastic. "I was a lot of help to you on the floor."

She laughed then; she couldn't help it. At the sound, Ryan lifted his head and smiled. "You think it's funny, do you? One sight of your blood and I lose five shades of color and plant my face in the floor."

Again she laughed, surprised at how good it felt. "You didn't quite fall all the way to the floor, Ryan. The nurse caught you."

"Oh, you're real funny, Doc." His thumb stroked her wrist, warming her skin, making heat flood her face. Then the amusement drained from his voice, though his eyes never left hers. "It was hard, hard to see you in such pain, Kayla. And with so much blood everywhere. It made me sick. And when I think of what we'd just done, of how we made love like we did, while you were hurting—"

"I was fine." Her voice shook.

"You never said a word." His fingers moved over her arm in soothing circles, coaxing a response from her as she leaned closer.

"It didn't hurt then," she admitted a little breathlessly. She pulled her hand from his and gave a last longing glance at those doughnuts.

"All you have to do," he drawled slowly, one corner of his wide, sexy mouth lifting up, "is admit that maybe, just maybe, you want to stay for dinner. And the doughnuts are yours. The ice cream too."

From the other room Lindsay laughed. Kayla's heart tumbled a little bit, and Ryan, watching her every move, caught on.

"You miss her."

"Yes."

"I offered you a solution to that."

She looked at him—a mistake. Those intense eyes of his leveled her. "Yes, you did."

"Change your mind?"

Yes, she wanted to cry, *I have changed my mind. Marry me, hold me, love me. Forever.* "You mean about marrying you for Lindsay's sake?"

He frowned. "You make it sound like a chore."

"I didn't do that, you did."

His eyes sparked with temper. "Fine. Again, don't marry me. Don't stay for dinner." He tucked his hands in his pockets. "I'll even make it easy and stop asking. But it's Lindsay's birthday Saturday. I'm having a picnic for her. You're welcome."

Damn him for making her feel small. "Of course I'll come."

Midway through the week, Kayla got called into administration. Waiting there for her were a dozen red roses in a crystal vase.

The card simply read MISS YOU, MATT.

She'd been avoiding him. He'd come by the hospital, her house, even once to the gym she sometimes used. Much as she tried, she couldn't restore the easy friendship they'd once shared.

But neither did she like knowing he hurt because of her.

To ease her heart, she made her way to Francine's room.

"They're moving me to the second floor," Francine announced happily. "A couple of weeks in long-term and I'll get to go home."

"Oh, Frannie, that's good." Kayla hugged her, silently fretting over her aunt's weight loss. "I'm so happy for you." But she thought of the attack and sobered.

"Too bad Ryan refuses to let me even think about it. He says I'm going to his beach house for a while."

"Good," Kayla said, swamped with emotion for the man who cared so much.

"Kayla . . ." Francine hesitated. "Did you ever read that diary I asked you about? Remember the one I found on my shelves? It's been bothering me."

"No, I never got a chance." Nor did she want to.

"I think you should. I remember finding it before you and Ryan came, and reading through it." She frowned.

Kayla looked at her aunt. "Do you remember something, Frannie? Something important?"

"No." She sighed, worrying her fingers together over her blanket. "I don't. I'm sorry. It's driving me crazy."

"Don't push it," Kayla said, giving her another hug and wishing she didn't look so feeble and vulnerable. "It'll come."

"Will you bring me that diary if you go to the cabin?" she asked.

"Yes. Please, don't worry, Frannie. Everything will come." Kayla hoped.

Tess was waiting for her at home with a box of pizza and a six-pack of soda. Ryan was keeping Lindsay that night at his house.

"Wow," Tess said, seeing Kayla alight from her car with the roses. "Ryan?"

She laughed a little. "Does Ryan seem the red-rose type to you?"

"No," Tess said dreamily. "He doesn't. He'd bring wildflowers, candles, and bath oil."

Kayla had to laugh again. "Probably." Her amusement died. "These are from Matt."

Tess went quiet for a minute. "You guys make up yet?"

"No."

She'd plowed her way through her half of the pizza when Tess asked her quietly, "Why is it so hard to believe that Ryan wants you for you?"

"Maybe because he doesn't," she said confidently. But that confidence wavered when Tess rolled her eyes. And again when Kayla thought back to how Ryan had looked at her the other night, with his eyes warming with affection and so much more.

After another piece, Tess groaned and stood. "I've gotta go, honey. It's late." She paused at the back door. "You coming on Saturday to Ryan's picnic?"

"I'll be there," she said, wondering how she'd get through the entire day without falling at the man's feet.

"Good girl," Tess said, smiling.

Kayla locked the door after her and wandered upstairs, still too keyed up to sleep. She spoke to Francine on the phone, then stepped out of her clothes.

Then she heard the creak.

She knew that sound all too well. Someone was in her house.

FOURTEEN

Kayla's hands shook as she shoved her arms in her robe, but this time she didn't hesitate. Grabbing the heavy policeman's flashlight from under her bed, she flipped off her light and ran to stand behind her closed door.

With her heart slamming against her ribs, she waited. All she could hear was her own harsh breathing and the drumming in her ears. When the handle to the door started to turn slowly, she wanted to panic.

Instead, she brought the flashlight up high over her head, preparing to swing down with a vengeance. She never got the chance. The door slammed open, and she was flung back against the wall, trapped.

Her head hit hard, and as she started to fall, the door smashed into her chest, knocking the air from her lungs. Falling, she lifted her head, gasping desperately for air that wouldn't come.

A bright light exploded inside her head, and she lost consciousness.

A moan woke her, her own. The darkness terrified her, and for a moment Kayla did panic, thinking she was blind.

The light was still off.

Dragging herself up on hands and knees, she fought the urge to throw up as her movement shot pain through her head. Somehow she managed to reach the lamp and flipped it on, crying out with the spearing pain the light caused her head.

When she could open her eyes again, confusion muddled her thoughts. *Blood on my robe again,* she thought distantly, smearing it with her fingers. *How did that happen?*

She stared helplessly at the phone, which seemed to loom miles away. The house creaked, a normal housey sort of sound, but she whimpered in fear, huddling into a ball and closing her eyes. Far too much a coward to lie there in the open, she crawled toward the phone.

Finally she got her shaky, blood-covered fingers on the receiver and . . . dropped it.

It was then she noticed the condition of her room. Shambles. Drawers opened, the contents dumped on the floor; the closet had been ransacked; her desk—the same one she'd just put back together—was ravaged. Clothes, papers, books, and shoes all covered her floor.

Standing wasn't an option, not with the screaming pain radiating through her head. Gritting her teeth, she managed to hold her head and the phone at the same time.

Later, when she tried to explain her reasoning to Tess, she couldn't. There was no logical reason why she called Ryan instead of 911. She blamed her fingers.

He answered on the third ring, sounding sexy, sleepy, and irritated.

She whispered because it hurt to talk. "Ryan, it happened again."

"Kayla?" came his suddenly alert voice. "What happened again?"

Wasn't that obvious? She wiped her forehead and her fingers came away bright red. "Never mind, I woke you. I'm sorry." Was that her voice? All whispery and slurred?

"Wait!" he said quickly. "Don't hang up. Tell me what happened again. Are you in trouble?"

Trouble. Now, why did he assume that? She'd never been in trouble, not until she'd met him anyway. Again her slick fingers dropped the telephone, and it slid on the carpeting. She stared stupidly at the receiver. Then she looked at her room again and remembered.

"Kayla," Ryan said firmly and swiftly when she brought the phone back to her ear. "Are you hurt?"

"I think so." Her words mixed together like a drunk, annoying her. "But you'd better stay there. Lots of blood. You'll faint." Her vision grayed.

"Don't move," he ordered. "I'm calling the police and the ambulance. I'm coming as fast as I can. Do you understand? Kayla? *Dammit, can you hear me?*"

The panic in his voice got through. "You're coming," she said obediently, leaning her pounding head back against the wall and closing her eyes. Fear found her. "Hope he's not still here."

She heard his frantic oath, the beep of his portable phone, and knew he was calling help as they spoke.

"Hang on, Kayla," he whispered. "Please, sweetheart, hang on."

Kayla stared at the interesting texture on her ceiling as she listened to his sure, controlled voice bark orders to dispatch on the other line.

"Kayla," he said urgently. "Lindsay and I are getting in my car. Can you hear me?"

"Yeah. You're shouting." Again her eyes closed. Blood ran down her neck. Her vision wavered and she fought unconsciousness one last time. "Hurry. My head's falling off."

It was difficult for Ryan to deal with this panic that welled so deep within him, dictating his every move. He'd never had much use for the emotion before Lindsay. Before Kayla. It was Kayla bringing that emotion out in him now.

He'd wasted an extra twenty minutes taking Lindsay to Tess's, but he hadn't wanted to bring the baby to the hospital, hadn't wanted to scare her.

Sprinting down the hospital corridor, he skidded to a stop in front of the nurses' station. The call he'd made from his car had told him Kayla was there, being treated for head trauma. They would tell him nothing else, and he could only hope she hadn't been hurt more than he knew. Panic filled him, thinking about it, even though he knew that she, being on her own turf, was in the best hands possible.

It didn't help.

The nurse refused him access even after he flashed his badge, and he was left to cool his heels pacing the hall until the doctor came out.

"You were asking about Dr. Davies." The tall, white-haired man looked at him cautiously. "I'm Dr. Chapman."

"Ryan Scott. How is she?"

"Are you a friend? You showed a badge, but the police were already here."

Regulations, Ryan thought with welling frustration. They wouldn't tell him a goddamned thing unless . . . "I'm her fiancé."

Well, he'd asked her, hadn't he?

The doctor's face brightened. "She didn't say a

word. Come with me. I'll have to check with her before I let you in, you understand."

"Yeah," he muttered. "I understand." What he understood was that he was about to be tossed out on his ear. He hovered between wanting her to be perfectly all right and wanting her to be out of it enough that he could finagle his way in to see her. "The officer told me she got hit over the head. How bad is she?"

"Nasty concussion. Several abrasions. We're going to keep her overnight. She's quite lucky."

Lucky, hell. Rage consumed him. Too many attempts and no lead. He needed a motive, a solution, and he needed it fast.

"Are there any other . . . injuries?" God, he could barely speak, could barely stand having his question answered. All sorts of horrors flitted through his mind.

"Not that we know of."

Okay, he thought, he could handle this. Probably just a concussion. *Just a concussion.* Jesus. She'd nearly died again. Because of his pride. He'd known, dammit, he'd known she was in danger, and he'd let his stupid, hurt ego get in the way. It wouldn't happen again.

So she didn't want to marry him. He could still keep her safe. Dr. Chapman entered Kayla's room, obviously expecting Ryan to be polite and wait outside.

Not being particularly polite or courteous, Ryan followed the doctor in. Kayla's eyes were closed, her head wrapped in gauze. Her skin lay hollow against her cheekbones, looking a little green, especially next to the hospital gown. Covered to the chest in a white blanket, he could make out the bulge of her IV line.

She looked so still, he wanted to cry.

Dr. Chapman touched her arm and called her name. When she didn't respond, Ryan's heart all but stopped.

He must have made a noise, because the doctor whirled around.

"You should have waited—" he started to say.

"Is she all right?" he cut in harshly.

The doctor came forward, took his arm, and turned toward the door. "You'll have to wait until she wakes up—"

"No," he said hoarsely. "Please."

The doctor hesitated, searching his face for a moment. "There will be a nurse in every few minutes. She'll try to kick you out. If you can convince her to stay, you deserve to."

Grateful for the short reprieve, Ryan sank to a chair by Kayla's bed. Softly, he stroked her arm, speaking to her in a low voice. He had no idea if she could hear him, but he talked anyway, telling her how smart he thought she was, how he admired her. If he stopped talking, he'd lose it. She looked like hell.

When she made a little sound and tried to bring her hand to her head, he gripped it tight and called her name softly.

Her lovely blue eyes flickered open, then slammed shut. "The light hurts," she whispered.

Jumping up, he turned off two of the three lights, then rushed back to her side. "Better?"

"Thirsty."

He scrambled to pour water from the pitcher by her bed, but when he brought the glass to her lips, he found she'd fallen asleep again. Sighing, he sat back down to wait.

When she whispered his name a minute later, he shot straight up. "I'm here." Wrapping his warm hands around her chilled one, he brought it to his mouth, kissing her fingers.

Her lips quirked in a faint smile, but her eyes remained firmly closed. "I didn't get lucky enough . . . to have my head fall off. It hurts."

He bowed his head, brushing his forehead against her hand. "God, Kayla. You scared me to death tonight. Shaved years off my life when I took that call, I swear."

A nurse came in, checked her vitals, and patted Kayla's other hand. "How ya doing?"

"Ready to make my rounds," she whispered.

"You didn't mention you had a handsome fiancé, Dr. Davies." The nurse looked him up and down and laughed. "But I guess I can understand the need to keep this one to yourself."

Kayla's eyes flashed open with alarming clarity as they focused on Ryan. But he'd been in the hot seat one too many times to let her daunting look bother him. He raised his eyebrows, silently daring her to contradict him. Evidently, she didn't have the strength, for after narrowing those lovely eyes on him, she just sighed and closed them. "I didn't want you to get jealous," she said to the nurse. "It's so hard to get a good, *honest* man nowadays."

The nurse laughed and Ryan squirmed. Once she was gone, Ryan stroked Kayla's arm again. Her breathing evened out and he thought she'd drifted off. He wondered how long she'd be allowed to sleep before she had to be woken. What if they forgot? Nerves had him reaching for the call button.

"I'm glad you came," Kayla whispered suddenly.

He took her hand. "Did you think I wouldn't?"

Slowly, deliberately, as if it caused her great pain, she turned her head toward him. He could see the dark circles beneath her eyes, could sense the bone-weariness of her. "It doesn't matter."

"I think maybe it does." He continued to stroke her skin. "I'll always be there for you, Kayla. Shame on you for thinking otherwise." He waited a minute. "Can you tell me what happened?"

Fear filled her eyes. She closed them and turned her head back away. "No."

Again rage and his own fear swirled within him until he thought he would spontaneously combust. He needed, badly, to smash something. Better yet, he wanted just five minutes with whoever had attacked her. Three, he thought. He could do it in three.

"Kayla sweetheart," he said, forcing his voice to be calm and gentle. "It'll help us find who it was if you tell me what you know. Did you see anything? Hear anything?"

"I went upstairs." She paused, and he could see her sorting out the events. He squeezed her hand.

"And then?" he pushed when she hesitated. She bit her lip. "Kayla?" The panic again, that chilling, helpless panic.

She closed her eyes. "I undressed."

She paused, and this time blushed furiously. He'd been a cop before a detective. He'd heard and seen it all, and more. But this was Kayla fighting humiliation and the memory of someone intruding, watching her when she'd thought she'd been alone. When she tried to turn her head away, he caressed her face with his fingers, bringing her back to face him.

"Kayla, you're safe now, I promise. Nothing else can happen to you, I won't let it."

"I heard a noise," she said quietly, her wide, hurt eyes open on his now. "I knew someone was out there, like before." She drew a shaky breath, and he smoothed back her curls from her face. "I grabbed my flashlight, turned off the lights, and waited behind the closed door."

"Good girl," he said, impressed by her quick thinking and bravery, shaken by what could have happened to her.

"I was shaking so bad, I didn't think I'd be able to hit anyone, but I didn't know what else to do."

"You did great," he said, thanking God she didn't have Lindsay with her this time. "You did everything right. What happened next?"

"The door slammed open and hit me. I couldn't breathe. I think I fell. Then I was hit over the head." She stopped abruptly, squeezing her eyes tight.

"Sweetheart, did he . . . hurt you after that?" He held his breath.

"No," she whispered. "I don't think so. After that I was alone."

"You didn't actually see anyone?"

"I don't remember much after that," she admitted.

She had indeed been lucky, just as the doctor had said. It could have been much, much worse. "Someone's looking for something," he managed to say quietly. "Do you remember calling me, Kayla?"

Opening her eyes, her lips curved slightly. "Vaguely."

Now that he'd seen that smile, he could tease. "Why do you suppose you called me first?" he wondered aloud, tracing her jawbone with his fingertips. She was so soft, he thought, so fragile. "Maybe because you were thinking of me?"

"I'm not up for stroking your ego right now, Ryan."

"Nine-one-one would have been faster, easier," he ventured, watching her as he caressed her face gently. He wanted so badly to hear her say how she needed him, wanted him. Then his insane need for her would be so much easier to take.

"Maybe I wasn't thinking," she murmured, only the faint blush giving her away. "Hey, Ryan?"

He dragged his gaze from her kissable lips and looked into her eyes.

There was faint amusement there. "If I show you my new stitches, will you faint for me again?"

She'd be the death of him yet.

Ryan was there the next morning when Kayla was discharged. Though she looked positively gray to him, she insisted she felt fine. He looked to the nurse for the truth.

"She's stubborn," the nurse said. "But I can guarantee you she's in pain. Just keep her quiet, get her lots of rest."

"I'm right here, Jeanne," Kayla said grumpily. "No need to talk as if I weren't. And I'm the doctor, remember?"

Jeanne just smiled patronizingly. "Yes, Dr. Davies, I know. But today you're my patient, so humor me."

Ryan smiled at Kayla's huff. When the nurse left, he asked, "Ready?"

"Who appointed you my caretaker?"

Ah, his little sweet Kayla. Sweet and cranky. "You're my fiancée, remember?"

Her sharp blue eyes narrowed. "I'm going to tell everyone I dumped you, so just forget it."

"You're losing a hell of a catch."

"Yeah, well, I'll take my chances." She relented ungraciously. "Fine. Take me out of here, Ryan."

He smiled and took her hand. Kissing it gently, he watched her eyes go cloudy with confusion, enjoying her racing pulse beneath his fingers.

"I'm taking you to my house," he said.

"No." She tried to tug her hand free, but he held

firm, kissing her again. Her pulse beat frantically. He almost smiled, but he was, after all, a very wise man.

"I'll call a taxi." She sounded a little desperate.

It was an empty threat, and he knew it. Fear still leapt in her eyes. But he didn't want her to come to him browbeaten. "Lindsay misses you," he said casually.

For a moment she ignored him, bending to fix her sandal, straightening her hair. "All right," she said finally. "But only because of Lindsay. I need a minute first."

"Good," he said brightly, matter-of-factly helping her to the bathroom. The minute the door shut behind her, his cheerful demeanor faded. His smile disappeared. She looked like hell and he was sick with worry. How was he going to keep her with him and find out what the hell was going on at the same time? Plus keep both her and Lindsay safe?

By the time they got to his house, Kayla was fast asleep, curled in her seat. Ryan opened her door and undid her seat belt, but when his arms went around her, she stiffened and shrieked.

"Shhh, Kayla," he murmured, holding her close. "You're okay now. I've got you. Remember?"

She nodded, her eyes still tightly shut against the bright daylight. He waited, holding her to him until her muscles relaxed and her heart rate slowed.

"I'm taking you inside."

"I'll walk," she protested, but didn't move.

Hoisting her up, he carried her inside, straight to his spare bedroom. By the time he'd spread the quilt over her, she was fast asleep again.

Tess stood with Lindsay in the doorway, watching worriedly. "If only I hadn't left her when I did—"

"Then you'd have been hurt too," he told her, tucking Kayla in, fretting over her pallor.

Lindsay smiled and pointed to Kayla. "Mama."

Ryan's gut tightened. "Yes, sweetheart. That's Mommy. But she's tired now. Let's let her rest, all right?"

"What's going to happen, Ryan?" Tess asked.

He had his ideas, but he needed proof. "It'll be over soon," he promised. He'd make sure of it.

Kayla woke up to a dark room, feeling like a new person. The sounds of the waves crashing over the shore reminded her where she was.

Ryan's house.

The clock said nine. She'd slept for nearly twelve hours. No wonder her stomach was growling.

Pushing away the ugly memories of being attacked, she forced herself to concentrate on the good.

Ryan had come when she needed him, offering her strength and protection. Maybe he'd offer food as well. Halfway to the door, she stopped, startled, and looked down at herself. She wore a large T-shirt, baggy sweatpants—neither belonged to her, but she'd have known that delicious male scent anywhere.

Who'd dressed her in Ryan's clothes?

She stopped to watch the gorgeous Lindsay slumbering peacefully in the next room.

Back in the hallway, she heard the rumbling of water mixed with a strange bubbling sound. Following it, she ended up on Ryan's upstairs deck, staring at the moon, feeling the ocean spray.

Inhaling the wonderful cold air, she tilted her head back and smiled at the sky scattered with brilliant stars. For the first time since her attack, her fear disappeared. Here she was safe.

"Kayla."

She whirled at the low, husky voice. Ryan sat in the hot tub on the far end of the deck, his long arms resting on the edge of the tub, watching her. Water drops dotted his wide, sleek shoulders, moonlight lit his hair like gold. He looked so good, so absolutely welcoming.

Maybe *she* was safe, but her *heart* sure wasn't.

"I didn't see you," she said inanely.

"How do you feel?"

Because her legs felt rubbery, she backed to a chair and tucked her bare feet beneath her. "Fine. I can't believe I slept so long."

"You needed it."

She found herself staring at him, at his bare chest, his wet hair, into those sharp, worried eyes that held such concern. In return he studied her quietly, his dark gaze steady. Her pulse tripped.

"I'm wearing your clothes."

"And they never looked so good." His eyes heated when they ran over her; then he patted the water next to him. "Come in?"

The water looked warm and inviting. So did the man in it, but he couldn't distract her so easily. "How did I come to be wearing these clothes, Ryan?"

He straightened and the level of the tub water dipped alarmingly down to his hard, flat stomach. "You don't remember, then?"

Was that amusement in his eyes? It couldn't be, wouldn't be if they had. . . . Relief had her sagging back. "If I did, would I be asking?"

Oh, he was very amused now. That grin spread. "Tess dressed you, Kayla. Not me. I had Lindsay."

"Oh."

"Disappointed?"

"In your dreams."

He laughed. "Come in here."

The water lapped at his perfect belly, played over his hips. His body was truly magnificent and hers was black and blue. "No," she said hastily, jumping up from her chair so quickly her vision wavered.

"Careful," he admonished her, rising. Water rained out. Tan skin flashed, followed by that particularly fantastic part of his anatomy which hadn't been exposed to the sun.

He wore nothing, nothing at all. Heat rose within her, that heat only he could cause, and when her knees went weak, she knew it had absolutely nothing to do with her injury.

"Kayla, wait."

"Don't!" She raised a hand to keep him in the tub. "Don't get out, I'm . . . fine." Whirling, she ran off the deck and back to the bedroom, diving under her covers.

How the heck was she supposed to resist that man?

FIFTEEN

In the morning Ryan found Kayla at his breakfast table, sipping tea. "Good morning," he said, strangely stirred by the sight of her wearing his clothes.

She frowned and mumbled.

His pleasure faded. "What's wrong?"

"Nothing."

"It's more than nothing," he insisted, taking a chair. Knowing she was always grumpy before she'd eaten, he took an orange from the fruit bowl on the table, peeled it, and handed it to her to eat. "Can I make you some breakfast?"

"Tess already did." But she popped an orange slice in her mouth anyway.

He thought he knew her well enough to tell what was bothering her. "You feel okay?"

"Fine."

"Lindsay okay?"

"She's great."

"Did you sleep all right?" He bit back his appreciative smile as she stormed to her feet.

"Oh, for heaven's sake," she exploded, glowering at

him. "I'm fine. Lindsay's fine. The bed's fine. It's just that—"

He rose, too, took her wrist, and tugged her closer. "It's just what, Kayla?"

"I can't stay here," she whispered, her sorrowful gaze meeting his. "I need to go to work. I need my clothes. I need my car. I want to go home, but . . ."

"You're frightened?" he asked softly, touching her face until she looked at him again. "Is that it?"

She said nothing.

He wanted to tell her what he suspected, how, if he were right, he'd have this whole thing over with soon, but he wasn't ready to do that. He'd taken one too many chances already and it had almost gotten her killed. "I can take you home now if you'd like. I'll wait for you and bring you back. That way you won't miss Lindsay's birthday picnic today."

"I'm fine to drive."

"No," he said firmly. She still looked like hell, and that bruise over her eye was going to haunt him. "I'm not leaving you alone in that house. If you don't want my company, I'll have a cop friend of mine take you, but you're not going by yourself."

The ocean outside his window seemed to fascinate her, and she didn't appear to be listening to a damn thing he said. No, he thought, she *was* listening, she just didn't want to.

"Kayla—"

"Fine," she said, sounding annoyed while looking vastly relieved. "But I don't want to hold you up. I'll take an escort."

His heart went out to her as he realized how scared she really was. It also twisted that she didn't want his company but the distant comfort of a stranger. "It'll soon be over, Kayla," he promised.

"Will it?" She turned doubting eyes to his. "I wonder."

Unbeknownst to Ryan, Kayla made a quick stop on the way to her house. Her undercover cop escort hadn't minded one bit, had even carried the contents of Lauren's security box from the bank to the car. But as she let herself into her own house, the diaries she'd found weighed heavily on her mind.

Why had her sister left her a box full of diaries? Exhaustion dictated she stop thinking about it, if only until she felt better. She set them down in her living room and went upstairs for a change of clothes. The doorbell rang.

It was her police escort and Matt.

"Kayla," Matt said, looking annoyed. "Will you please tell this nice officer that I'm harmless? He seems intent on keeping me away and—"

Kayla moved a hand to her aching head, feeling so tired, she wanted to cry. She'd promised Ryan she'd grab some things and head straight back to his house, but she was suddenly too sleepy to do that. All she wanted was to curl up in bed and sleep.

Matt stepped over her threshold, touching her shoulders. "Kayla," he said, worry weighing down his voice. "What is it?" He pointed to her head. "What's happened?"

"You okay here, Dr. Davies?" the officer broke in, wearing a frown and staring at Matt. "I was told not to let anyone in."

"I'm fine," she said, then looked at Matt. "But I really need to be alone right now—"

"Shhh," Matt whispered. "He'll kick me out. I just need to talk to you for a quick second."

Kayla swallowed her sigh and reassured the officer. Matt led her into the kitchen and pushed her into a chair.

"Let me get you a drink," he said.

"Matt—"

"It's all gone bad for me this week," he interrupted, waving his elegant hands. "I've fallen apart and need your help."

Kayla had to hide an ironic smile. Matt lived in a perpetual state of crisis, and she'd come to learn how totally self-centered he could be, unable to believe anyone's problems could be as big as his own. She didn't know if it was the actor in him, or just the Hollywood kid, but it annoyed her now. "It's been a pretty bad week for all of us, Matt."

"Yeah?" He glanced at her sharply. "You didn't tell me what happened to you. You were hurt."

"It's a long story." And one she didn't want to relive just yet. "But I'm fine now." If only she didn't feel like she was about to collapse.

"Hey," he said casually, "did you ever go through Lauren's box?"

"As a matter of fact, I did. I found her old diaries."

"Kayla."

She whirled at the familiar, deep voice. Ryan filled the doorway wearing a dark look that matched his black chambray shirt. The long sweep of his black jeans added to that vengeful, dangerous look.

A tingling sense of apprehension shivered up her spine, and she pushed out of her chair. "Ryan," she began uneasily, but his narrowed eyes were on Matt as he moved into the kitchen.

Matt straightened. "Maybe you'd better call off your watchdog before he bites," he suggested to Kayla.

"Get out," Ryan said in a quiet voice of steel.

Kayla wanted to tell Ryan to knock it off. She wanted to tell Matt to stop baiting Ryan. She wanted them both to leave so she could collapse in peace. But Kayla had discovered things rarely happened exactly as she wanted.

Her vision faded around the edges and the rest blurred.

"Kayla," she heard Ryan's voice say from very, very far away. The black spread inward until she could see nothing.

Warmth and fuzziness prevailed. Kayla held still, unwilling to disturb that delicious feeling of security. Then that protective heat shifted and she realized she was in someone's arms. She had no problem detecting whose they were.

"Proof will be difficult," Matt was saying.

"Temporary setback," Ryan admitted tightly.

The back door opened and shut, and Ryan made an indecipherable noise as Matt must have left. She opened her eyes to see Ryan anxiously staring down at her. Sighing with relief, he hugged her to him and rocked her slowly, letting out a deep breath.

"Tell me I didn't faint," she said, her voice muffled against his shirt. She closed her eyes and savored him holding her.

"All right," he said evenly, getting to his feet with ease. "I've had enough of your stubborn attempts to prove you're fine." He strode from the kitchen and, without breaking stride, continued out the front door. "You don't even slightly resemble fine, and I don't want to hear it anymore." With a gentleness that belied his hard tone, he placed her in the passenger seat, his hands lingering on her waist.

Then he ruined the tender moment by slamming the door.

Leaning down, he placed his strained face in the open window. "You've got two seconds to tell me what you want from the house—or you'll wear my clothes and like it."

He looked so absolutely fierce, it became a struggle not to giggle. "I have a duffel bag on my bed. That's all I need."

"Fine," he clipped, and stalked off, returning less than a minute later.

After five minutes of silence in which Ryan concentrated on driving the overcrowded, traffic-ridden freeways of Southern California, Kayla spoke.

"Why did you come to the house?"

"I never should have let you go," he retorted, deftly changing three lanes, then freeways, heading for Newport. His anger vibrated between them. "You look like hell."

"Thanks."

"You realize now that we're even." Suddenly, he grinned, relieving the harsh lines etched in his face. "You fainted dead away, sweetheart, no denying it." His grin spread, and as always, she was transfixed by the sight. "And *I* didn't pass out into your waiting arms."

She ignored him. "What did Matt mean when he said you couldn't prove a thing?"

His grin disappeared and his gaze flew to hers. "Where did you hear that?"

"After I passed out."

"Maybe you were dreaming."

"I don't think so." She studied him. "You said it was a temporary setback."

"Now I know you've been watching too much television."

She knew what she'd heard and yet . . . She studied him carefully, noticing the casual way he held the wheel, the easy, relaxed way his long body fitted into his seat. He gave her a harmless look and suddenly she wasn't sure. Could she have truly dreamed the entire thing?

Because it hurt to think, she sighed and closed her eyes. Then she felt the car stop and knew they were at his house. Ryan's fingers stroked her cheek, and because they felt so good, so cool, she turned her face into them.

"You feel so hot," he murmured, moving closer.

"There's something you're not telling me, Ryan." But she was so tired, it had become an effort to talk.

His fingers remained on her. The air in the car shifted, became tight, intimate. "Kayla," he whispered, "do you trust me?"

It was hard not to, with those fingers sweeping over her face and neck, with those dark, fathomless eyes on hers. He took a handful of hair and stared at it reverently, but his jaw was tight, his thoughts elsewhere.

Suddenly aware that he knew exactly what was going on, and that he wasn't talking, she straightened. "You *know*, Ryan, I'd bet every last penny I have on it."

His eyes met hers, but he said nothing.

"Tell me."

"Trust me," he said urgently. "Say you do."

She couldn't help herself. "I do."

A sigh escaped him. She opened her mouth to push him for more, but his lips covered hers, and any arguments she might have had escaped her as he moved his mouth purposely, driving away her exhaustion, her protest, her every thought but his warm, giving body.

The texture of his lips fascinated her. So did the roughness of his hands as they moved tenderly up her spine, then streaked under her shirt, evoking shivers he promptly soothed away.

The man could kiss, she thought vaguely, allowing him to pull her closer. She could taste the heat, the reckless lust that drove him, but there was much more. Warmth, affection, intense hunger, *all for her.* Helplessly, unbelievably aroused, she gripped the taut muscles of his shoulders and held on for dear life.

She trembled with need and passion, with heat and yearning, and he dragged his mouth from hers to bury his face in her neck.

When his breathing had evened out a little, he said, "You remember what happened in your kitchen."

"You mean when I fainted dead away into your arms?" She smiled self-consciously, smoothed down the shirt she wore. "You're lucky you didn't break something when you carried me all the way to your car."

"You're not heavy," he said so sharply, she lifted her head to stare at him. He squeezed her thigh, ran his eyes down her luscious body, watching as it quivered. He longed to do more than look, but he was quickly running out of time. "You have a body most women would die for—are you listening to me?" She'd turned away.

"Hard to miss it," she said dryly. "You're shouting again."

He caught the pleased glow of her cheeks. "I'm not. You're distracting me. Kayla, what diaries? I heard Matt ask you about what you'd found."

"Oh! I forgot about them." She gave him a trusting, open look that melted him. She really did trust him, he thought, his heart soaring. Surely that was the first step.

"Lauren kept diaries," she said, telling him what he already knew. "For some reason, she left them to me. I've never read them, but they're at my house."

God. The diaries. Why hadn't he seen it sooner?

He'd had his proof all along and did not even realize it.

———————————

Lindsay giggled and dove into her cake with the appreciation of a connoisseur. Francine, from her perch in a wheelchair, laughed. From behind her camera, Kayla laughed too. "Well, baby, you didn't understand blowing out the candle, but you got this part down pat. Smile, honey, smile for me."

"Mama," Lindsay said, giving her a chocolate grin. Then she looked at Ryan and reached her sugar-coated hands out for him. "Dada."

Everyone stopped and stared at her. The camera shook in Kayla's hands.

"Dada," Lindsay repeated more loudly, less patiently.

Ryan's mouth had fallen open. He shifted stunned eyes to Kayla. "Did you hear that? She said—"

"I know," Kayla whispered, her heart swelling at the pure joy on his face. "She said daddy."

Ryan snatched the one-year-old and hugged her close. Frosting smeared across his shirt, his cheek, and Kayla raised the camera, but she never snapped the shot, lost in the love flowing between father and daughter. No matter what it had cost her, she thought, this moment was worth every bit of it.

Lindsay grabbed Ryan's cheeks and touched her nose to his. "Dada," she said again. "Dada."

Ryan drew a shuddery breath and rubbed his nose to hers. Kissing her loudly, he looked up at Francine, Tess, and Kayla with suspiciously bright eyes. "Wow," he said, slapping a hand to his chest. "That'll get to you."

No, Kayla thought, her eyes glued to his. *You get to me.*

It wasn't until a bit later that the emotional events of the day caught up with Kayla. In Ryan's bathroom she kneeled before the tub, giving Lindsay her bath. She looked down at the happy girl playing with bubbles, and her insides ached.

Soon she'd have to face her own house again.

Ryan and Lindsay would go on with their lives without her.

The tears welled unexpectedly, and she sat back on her heels, swiping at them. She'd cried more lately than she had in her entire lifetime. Weary of fighting, she let the tears go.

"Wearing out your mommy, I see." Ryan stood in the doorway, and for a long, telling moment his gaze met hers. Then he squatted down to the tub and lifted out a slippery, squealing Lindsay. "Silly girl," he said, smiling. "Don't you know that's a no-no?"

Without another glance in Kayla's direction, he wrapped up his daughter in a towel and left the room. Knowing she should rise, Kayla sniffled but didn't move. She didn't have the energy. At least Ryan hadn't seemed to notice her pathetic lapse into self-pity.

He'd called her Lindsay's mommy. Cruelly, she dashed out the thread of hope that that inspired. He hadn't meant it.

He hadn't meant a lot of things. His marriage proposal had been out of a sense of decency, a need to keep a family life together for Lindsay. He certainly didn't love her. How could he after what she'd put him through?

She could have said yes, but it would have killed her to live a mockery of a marriage when she so badly wanted the real thing—with him.

Then gentle hands pulled her up, Ryan's hands, bringing her to stand in front of him. "Kayla," he said in an achingly tender voice. "Sweetheart, don't cry." The pads of his thumbs wiped her tears away. "There's so much we have to talk about, but we have to do something else first. Come with me?"

She let him lead her downstairs without protest, unbearably touched by the light of affection in his gaze. At his car she hesitated. "But—"

"Tess and Francine will watch Lindsay," he said, pulling into the street.

"What are we doing?"

"The diaries, Kayla. We have to have them." He was on the freeway, driving too fast. "Then we'll have forever to talk about the rest."

"The rest?"

"Us." He let that settle, then looked at her. "Kayla, I don't think your sister killed herself. Those diaries are going to prove that she was murdered, and that the murderer is now stalking you."

"*What?*"

His glance was sympathetic but steely. "He thinks you can identify him."

This was going too fast; she didn't understand. Or didn't want to. "This is ridiculous." She placed a hand to her suddenly aching head.

"Kayla, listen to me." He paused to whip around a slower truck. "We'll get through this. But until we get those diaries, you're in danger."

"Diaries." Her blood went cold as she remembered. "Oh, my God."

"What? What is it, Kayla? What did you remember?"

The urgency in his voice told her exactly how serious he was about this situation, how much he did truly believe she was in trouble. His eyes were filled with fear and concern, and it was for her. Nothing could have reached her more. "Francine's been talking about a diary—she read one of them."

His mouth went grim. "We have to have them."

"Why would the diaries identify Lauren's murderer?"

He hesitated, making a show of getting off the freeway and navigating onto the busy four-lane highway.

Dammit, he was holding back with her. *"Ryan."*

"She knew him," he said with a sigh, turning into her quiet neighborhood.

He didn't have to say the rest. Lauren had known him and now so did she. And that person was the one who'd twice tried to kill her. The memory of being attacked in her bedroom had her slamming her eyes shut and gripping the dash.

With a sound of compassion and understanding, Ryan reached for her, squeezing her thigh. "It's going to be all right," he promised solemnly. "It'll be over as soon as we get proof." Pulling into her driveway, he turned and hugged her trembling body fiercely. "I won't let anything else happen to you," he whispered, kissing her brow. "I promise."

It helped, having those warm, possessive arms around her. But she didn't point out her next thought, that her stalker had gotten to her twice already.

Inside her house, she led Ryan to the couch where she'd dropped the box of diaries.

They were gone.

"I left them here," she said, feeling sick. "I know I did. Then you came and we left in a hurry."

"And now they're gone. Damn." He stared at her in dismay for one second before grabbing her arm. At the car he pushed her gently in and ran around to the driver's side. "We'll have to hurry."

"Hurry?"

"There's one diary he didn't get, one I forgot all about until just now."

"That's right," Kayla breathed. "Francine asked me to get it for her."

"It's in the cabin's library." His glance was intimate, loving, and left her with a huge lump in her throat. "I'm sorry," he said. "I know you're tired. But buckle up. We're going to Lake Mead."

For the thousandth time, Ryan glanced over the sleeping Kayla. Having her sleep the entire drive had been handy. One, she desperately needed the sleep; and two, he wasn't ready to face her questions.

If she'd been feeling like herself, she would have guessed what was happening by then.

And she'd be even more terrified. He hated seeing that fear glimmering in her blue eyes, hated even more knowing he himself had put some of that there.

She deserved better, and he planned on making sure she got it.

Darkness had long since descended over the desert by the time he stopped the car in Francine's driveway. One glance at Kayla told him she was out like a light, and by the looks of her tense, exhausted face, she wasn't having peaceful dreams.

Knowing she'd object didn't stop him from bending over her and kissing her softly on those lips he loved. When he smoothed back her hair, something deep stirred within him, more than protectiveness, more than lust, more than simple compassion.

It was love. And it hurt like hell.

"Be right back," he whispered, kissing her again. She didn't budge, not even when he shut the door.

He'd just grab that diary and come right back.

Or so he thought.

⊰────────⊱

She couldn't breathe. Kayla woke abruptly, fighting the smothering feeling, striking out at the hands that covered her nose and mouth.

Cold, hard metal was jammed against her neck and a hand gripped the front of her shirt. "Do exactly as I tell you and you won't get hurt," came the low, hoarse voice. "Understand?"

Gripped by panic and fear, Kayla nodded. Then she was yanked from the car.

Where was Ryan?

"I want you to tell me where the last diary is," the gravelly voice said. "Tell me and I'll leave you alone."

"I don't know."

Silence was followed by a sharp jab in Kayla's back with a gun, forcing her to walk. "So you're going to be difficult to the end. Dammit. It didn't have to be this way."

The night was dark. The sound of water lapping against the dock came to her, as did the faint outline of the boat.

Where was Ryan?

Unsure, she hesitated at the water's edge, her head still aching unbearably.

"Move," came the hissing, angry voice. It sounded eerily familiar. "Now."

Dizziness hit her, but the sound of the gun cocking had her scrambling forward.

"Get in the boat. We're going for a little ride."

A ride. She turned her head to look over her shoulder, but was propelled forward by another push. Then yet another as she climbed on the boat, and she landed heavily on the bottom, scraping her hands and knees.

"I'll get that last diary myself," the hard voice said.

Recognition stopped her heart.

"I've had enough waiting for you. The rest of these diaries are going overboard, just where Lauren did."

A bag of the diaries was tossed to her feet.

"I'll save Matt's sorry hide myself, and then he'll have me to thank for his freedom."

Shoving her hair from her face, Kayla looked up. It had started to rain. Through that and her fierce headache she managed to see. Standing over her, wearing black and holding a gun aimed directly at her, was Tess.

"I really wish you hadn't looked," Tess said.

SIXTEEN

With a groan Ryan pushed to his feet, rubbing the back of his aching head.

Someone had hit him.

He scanned the shelves anxiously, sagging in relief when he spotted the diary. Then he took off running down the hall and out the front door, his heart in his throat.

But he was too late.

His car was empty. Kayla was gone.

A movement caught the corner of his eye, and he ducked, watching the two shadows work their way toward the dock. Kayla and a dark figure—Tess?

What the hell was she doing here, and who was with Lindsay?

Quietly, stealthily, Ryan moved closer, keeping low.

He had to bite his tongue as he watched Tess shove Kayla into the boat. He knew Tess had a gun. He had the lump on his head to prove it. Well, at least she hadn't killed him.

He pulled out his own gun, the one he'd been carry-ing ever since the drive-by incident, and dropped the diary down his shirt. Then he crept down toward the water's edge, hoping, praying.

Even in the darkness Ryan had no trouble seeing Kayla's huge, wide eyes, and he moved as close as he dared, praying for one good shot at Tess.

But Kayla was between them, and he couldn't risk it.

"Drive," Tess told Kayla, dragging her to her feet. "I'll direct you."

"I don't know how to drive the boat," came her quiet, shaky voice.

No, Kayla, Ryan thought bleakly, she'll know that's a lie.

Tess slapped Kayla so hard across the face, she whirled as she fell. "Don't lie," Tess snapped. "Not when I'm feeling this desperate."

I'm going to kill her, Ryan thought, his hands fisted in helpless rage. *With pleasure.* Taking advantage of the noise, Ryan slipped into the cold water, not daring to use the dock. Slowly, so he didn't ripple the water, Ryan moved forward.

Rain fell, giving him an even better advantage.

"Drive," Tess repeated, raising her voice. "I know you can."

Touching her reddened face, Kayla stared at Tess in shock. Ryan could see that her lips were blue and she shook uncontrollably. God, she was wet, he realized, and the air was freezing. He knew exactly how cold she was, since he'd gone numb from the water himself. Yet another reason to enjoy killing Tess.

"I can't believe you're doing this," Kayla said slowly, her teeth chattering. "I trusted you with Lindsay."

"You can still trust me with Lindsay. I'd never hurt that baby. She's sleeping peacefully, with Francine watching her. I followed you and Ryan, knowing you would lead me to the last diary."

"Why?"

Tess snorted indelicately and kicked the bag of diaries, giving Ryan more noise in which to use to his advantage. He edged closer. A few more feet and he could reach the boat.

"I didn't want you to find out. I thought I could keep this from you. But I love him," Tess said simply, sadly. "Sick. But it's the truth."

"Who?" Kayla asked. "You love who?"

"Matt."

"Oh, my God."

"Lauren wrote about him, you know. Wrote terrible, damning things, things that could put him away forever. You know, I really wanted to regret Lauren's death because it caused you so much pain, but it's hard to do that when I know what kind of a person she was. Don't feel bad about her anymore," Tess said solemnly. "Or Matt. I promised to help him."

"What things?" Kayla asked, her voice hitching. "What things in the diary?"

"Nothing you'd understand. Your life is perfect."

"It's not," she said with a shake of her head. "You know it's not."

"No point in discussing it now that I've gone this far. As soon as I destroy the diaries, we're done. I'll have protected Matt to the end, more than anyone could ask. Then I'll have him as my own, finally."

"Your own?" Kayla said weakly, wrapping her arms around her middle.

"Thankfully, you never really wanted him, so I don't have to deal with that."

Kayla stared at her, her face lit with confusion, horror.

"He did screw up, though," Tess said. "Remember that little incident you had on the road up here weeks ago? When you almost went over the cliff? I really laid into him for that stupid mistake. He was just trying to scare you into needing him, but he nearly killed you. I was furious."

"You were—" Kayla stopped short, her eyes wide. "My God."

"Then he messed up again, with Francine." With a wry shake of her head, she said, "You're probably wondering what I see in him, but he's the one for me, Kayla."

"Matt?"

"I'm sorry about Ryan."

Ryan heard Kayla's breath catch, heard his name tumble from her lips in an agonizing whisper.

Matt rose up from where he'd been crouched in the front passenger seat, moving close to a despondent Kayla. "Yeah, she killed him. And it was a treat to watch, believe me."

The sound of Kayla's weeping came over the water. Ryan reached the boat, aimed, then hesitated when Kayla stood abruptly and grabbed Tess's shoulders.

"*You* shot at Ryan that time in the car. You could have killed Lindsay!"

"I never intended to kill anyone," Tess said evenly. "I just wanted to scare Ryan off the track. He was getting close with all his snooping around. I wouldn't have hurt Lindsay. You've got to know that."

"You said you loved Lauren," she cried, dropping her hands from Tess and turning to Matt. "You *loved* my sister."

Matt laughed down into Kayla's tear-streaked face. "Never. It was the other way around. She was an extra on my set. So beautiful, so easy to manipulate. I made a bet with my lover that I could seduce her in less than a week. She was already married and three weeks pregnant, though I didn't know it. The challenge was too much to resist, Kayla."

"That's sick, setting out to ruin her life without a thought to the consequence," she said with disgust, turning from him, but to Ryan's frustration, Kayla remained in his way.

"She became obsessed with me," Matt said, "following me everywhere, saying she loved me. Women do that." He ignored Tess, and the way she'd turned to him, her mouth dropping open in surprise.

"Why didn't you just tell her to leave you alone?" Kayla asked.

He smiled and shrugged. "It suited me and my reputation. People believe I'm quite the lady's man, you know. And that's not an easy reputation to keep."

"What do you mean about other women?" Tess demanded, stepping closer to Matt. "How many have there been since we met?"

"None," Matt said with a sweet, innocent smile. He touched her face. "None as good as you, darling."

Kayla just stared at them in horror.

Ryan swore silently and shifted in the water, trying to get into a better position. He could feel Tess's climbing anger and impatience and he knew he had to hurry.

Kayla seemed to have trouble thinking clearly. "So you killed Lauren," she said to Matt. "And you," she said to Tess, "are protecting him."

"I love him," Tess said, her voice not nearly as confident as it had been. "He can't go to jail."

"But he killed Lauren!" Kayla said urgently. "He killed her simply because she got in his way."

Matt grabbed Kayla's hair and yanked her close, smiling down into her terror-filled face. "And because it was fun, Kayla. She was so desperate for love, approval, and she could get it from us."

"Us?"

He glanced at Tess briefly. "My lover and me. Before you, of course."

Ryan saw the exact moment the truth registered on Kayla's white face.

"You're gay," Kayla whispered.

Tess jerked in surprise, then her eyes narrowed. "You're—my God." She laughed wildly. "Is it true?"

Matt scowled.

"You've used me as you used Lauren," Tess said quietly, her eyes murderous.

Kayla brought her hands to her temples. "What happened, Matt? Did Lauren threaten to expose your all-American-boy image?"

Matt pouted, a ridiculous sight on the six-foot-plus man. "I didn't want my public to know. They'd never understand. I'd have been ruined."

"Instead, you ruined her."

"And me," Tess said quietly, lifting the gun in her hand and pointing it at Matt's chest. "I ought to shoot you."

But Matt still held Kayla close, too close, thought Ryan darkly. He still couldn't move without alerting them to his presence, and he couldn't shoot without risking Kayla's life.

"Now, Tess baby," Matt said with a cajoling smile. "You're jumping to conclusions here."

"Am I?" she asked softly, stepping closer. "I've given up my life for you, Matt. Threatened people I cared about, just to keep you safe. All in the name of love. But I think that you're using me."

"I'm not," Matt said, not letting go of Kayla. "You're a part of me, Tess, really."

Ryan hoped to God she didn't believe a word of this.

"But when I couldn't find Lauren's diaries after her

death," Matt said, "I started with Kayla." He caressed Kayla's cheek while Tess's jaw tightened.

"Matt—"

He ignored her. "So lovely, so reserved," he said to Kayla. "So unlike Lauren. I wouldn't have gotten far with that bet with you, would I have, Kayla?"

Kayla slapped his hand away and he laughed, still holding her hair. "I waited forever for you to trust me, Kayla. Too long. It's a shame it's come to this."

"It doesn't have to," she said urgently, trying to pull back. "People announce their sexual preferences all the time these days; no one cares."

"I care," said Tess, frowning. "I care a lot. You've really messed with me, Matt. You'll pay. Let her go."

"Changing sides?"

"Getting smart," Tess corrected Matt. "Let her go."

Matt didn't release Kayla. "Don't screw this up now, Tess. No one wants to idolize a junkie, much less a gay one, and that's what the public will see if we let them get a hold of this story."

"Let her go," Tess said, "or they *will* get a hold of this story, regardless."

"You're forsaking me?" Matt asked her in surprise. "Now? But you're already in too deep."

"Doesn't matter," Tess decided. "You're not worth it. Back up."

"No," Matt said stubbornly, lifting up his own gun and pressing it to Kayla. "Drive the boat."

"No," she cried, trying to pull back, but Matt dragged her to the wheel, keeping her as a shield.

Ryan gripped the edge of the boat, thankful for something more than the dark night. The boat was a jet engine, not a prop—which would have ripped him to shreds.

Matt jammed the gun into Kayla's ribs and said, "Go."

Tess lifted her hands, gripping the gun. "No!"

But Kayla started the boat, and Ryan rose out of the freezing water. Everyone whipped around at the sudden shift in the boat, and Kayla gasped, her eyes lighting up with hope and joy. Tess lifted her gun to Matt just as he raised his gun to shoot Ryan. At that exact moment Kayla took her hands from the wheel and dove at Matt, knocking both of them hard to the floor.

Tess screamed.

Ryan sprinted forward, heart in his throat, reaching them just as Matt's gun discharged.

"No!" Ryan shouted as both bodies went still.

SEVENTEEN

Ryan sat on the table in the emergency room, swinging his feet impatiently as the doctor checked the lump on his head. "How's Kayla?" he demanded.

"Fine," the doctor said distractedly, probing the wound with fingers that had Ryan wincing.

Fine. The woman had remained silent the entire drive back to Los Angeles, refusing to be checked out in any hospital but her own. But she'd been attacked for the third time, there was no way she could be fine. "You sure?"

"Yes." Dr. Chapman gave him a sympathetic look. "She told me she called off the engagement. I'm sorry."

Ryan grinned. She'd threatened to say that, and if she had, it meant she was fine indeed. He knew he would never get over the mind-numbing terror of nearly losing Kayla before his very eyes. When the gun had gone off in Matt's hands after Kayla had pounced on him, he'd nearly had a coronary trying to figure out who'd been shot.

He'd never forgive himself for putting Kayla in the situation of having to fight for her very life, *never*. Just as he'd never stop regretting that all Matt had gotten was a shot in the leg, but with the diaries it would be some time before he was free to worry about his reputation again.

Tess, too, even though she'd tried her best to keep Kayla safe.

Thankfully, Lauren had written in detail about the man she'd been obsessed with. She'd written about Matt's love life, naming more than a few stars whose own reputations would suffer. She'd also written about his extensive drug habits—buying *and* selling.

Francine, bless her nosy little heart, had read the diary and knew she had to keep Kayla safe from Matt. If only she'd told Ryan the entire truth from the beginning, a lot of trouble could have been avoided.

And maybe, Ryan thought thoughtfully, he would never have fallen in love.

Kayla walked into his cubicle then, startling Ryan from his thoughts. "You okay?" she asked with a weary smile.

He remembered the sight of her tackling Matt so he couldn't shoot him. The reasoning behind that stunned him. "Yeah, I'm okay." He stared at the woman who valued his life more than her own, unable to take his eyes off her. His heart squeezed painfully at the thought of what could have happened, and he had no one to blame but himself.

Looking at her, he came to the dazzling realization that he'd completely and truly gotten over what she'd done. She'd taken Lindsay and it no longer mattered. He wanted both ladies in his life—for keeps. Holding out a hand, he asked, "How about you? You okay?"

"Yes." Her little smile faded as she let him pull her down beside him. "Ryan, why didn't you tell me about Matt and Tess as soon as you knew?"

"I didn't know about Tess." Which gave him another bad moment. How could he have been such a bad judge of character? Thank God Tess had been blinded by love, not struck stupid. She'd come through in the end, though that wouldn't help her much in the law's eye.

Kayla gave him a long look. "You knew about Matt."

He should have told her. "Would you have believed it?"

"Maybe," she said. "But it would have been nice if you'd trusted me enough to try."

She looked as though she'd been through a battle, and she had. She'd lost her best friend. She had thought she'd lost him. Had nearly lost her life. That gorgeous hair he loved so much was tangled, her glorious blue eyes that showed her every emotion screamed exhaustion, and her creamy skin looked almost translucent. How could he explain to this woman who meant so much to him that he *did* trust her, far more than he wanted to admit? That all he wanted to do was protect her, love her?

She'd turned from him, unwilling to hear more, and he sighed.

"I hear you have a nasty bump on your head," she said, walking to the door. "No blood." She gave him a ghost of a smile, tears shimmering in her eyes. "Just as well," she whispered, "it was your turn to faint."

Tears? "Kayla?" He stood, cursing his wobbly legs, but she just shook her head. Those incredible eyes of hers looked at him, drenched.

"What—" he started to say.

But she just shook her head again and went through the door, leaving him staring after her in surprise, wondering.

And hoping.

The clock said two A.M. Unable to sleep, Kayla made her way out to Ryan's deck. He'd insisted she come to his house for one more night, not wanting her to go home so late by herself.

At least the night was a good one, she thought. The moon had risen, and silvery clouds floated across it. The sea was wild with an incoming storm, the crashing waves sounding in perfect harmony with the wind whistling across the beach.

She pushed her hair from her face and leaned over the edge.

"You look so beautiful out here."

At the sound of the achingly familiar voice, her heart took off, galloping in her chest. Her every muscle tightened as she clenched the railing, yearning, aching . . . needing.

"Why were you crying here today before we left for the lake?" Ryan asked quietly, coming up beside her.

She closed her eyes so she didn't have to see how good he looked in sweatpants and nothing else, all gorgeously tousled. Her hands tightened on the wood so she wouldn't reach for him.

"Tell me," he whispered, moving close enough that she could feel his body heat seep into her side, her legs. His bare chest brushed her arms.

She lowered her head, feeling his eyes on her.

"Kayla." He lifted her face in gentle hands, turning her toward him. His eyes were dark and serious. "Is it because you think you should leave?"

Without warning, her eyes filled. "I'm really sick of crying," she muttered.

"You don't have to leave, Kayla." His hands caressed

her face, his eyes searched hers. "I told you that. Stay with us forever. Marry me."

She gulped back her sudden sob, knowing he couldn't possibly understand how it hurt to hear him say that without the accompanying words she was dying to hear.

"Please," he said, "say you will."

"Why, Ryan?" She looked at him. "Tell me why you want me to marry you."

"There's Lindsay," he started to explain, stumbling over his words a little. His eyes turned troubled, nervous.

And suddenly it hit her with the force of a blow. How could she have not seen it sooner? He was just as afraid as she was . . . and cared just as deeply.

"As much as Lindsay matters," she said, buoyed by hope, "we can't marry for her. And you know what? After Lauren, I don't believe you would." She paused meaningfully. "So the question remains. Why should we marry, Ryan?"

The torturous glaze to his eyes gave her strength, cheered her on as nothing else could have. With the patience of a saint, she waited, her exhaustion suddenly gone.

"It . . . it would make us a family," he said in a slow, halting voice that told her exactly how much she'd unbalanced him.

It was a pleasure to see him less than one hundred percent confident and in control, but she simply nodded thoughtfully. "It would. But we're already sort of related. Aren't you my brother-in-law?"

He blanched. "I'm not your brother."

She prayed that the love in their hearts was enough to overcome the damage inflicted by their past. "No," she said softly. "You're not my brother."

"Kayla."

She raised her eyes at the impatient tone, a little smile on her lips, her heart pounding wildly. "Did you know your southern accent really comes out when you're upset? You sound just like a cowboy. There's so much I don't know about you, Ryan. So much I'd like to learn."

"Marry me, dammit." His eyes were desperate, so needy, she almost gave in—*almost.*

"Why?"

He looked at her then, and she knew he couldn't help but see the glimmer of hope and excitement, the amused nerves written all over her face. She couldn't hide it.

He stared, his eyes narrowed, then slowly, as he caught the truth, he smiled a deep, sexy smile that lit up his face. "Marry me because I love you, dammit," he said easily. "I don't know why I thought you didn't want to hear it, or why I thought I had to come up with every other reason under the sun, but I do love you, Kayla Davies."

Her sigh of relief echoed across the night.

He took her in his arms.

"Tell me again," she whispered.

"I love you," he said fiercely. "I love the way you love Lindsay, I love how you wear your heart on your sleeve for the whole world to see. I love your smile. I love the way you chew your cheek when you're nervous . . . like you're doing right now."

Laughing a little, she rested her head on his chest, enjoying his solid, if a little accelerated, heartbeat.

"I love everything about you," he told her steadily, "but then, you know that. So marry me." He leaned back to look at her. "What do you say?"

"I say . . . yes." She hesitated, wanting him to

know her acquiescence had nothing to do with what she was about to tell him. "Ryan, there's more."

"God, I hope so." His hands were on her.

"No, I mean—" She smiled nervously. "I'm going to have a baby. Your baby."

His hands stilled, then moved slowly to her still-flat belly. "You're—" His hand caressed her softly. "My baby."

"I'm not sure if it was the boat or the table." She blushed wildly, then laughed nervously, not knowing how he felt.

"Oh, Kayla," he whispered reverently, easing her heart instantly. "It's perfect. *You're* perfect."

"You might not feel that way when you have a toddler *and* a newborn."

"Yes, I will," he vowed. Then his eyes widened. "Are you okay? Is everything okay?"

She knew he worried about what she'd been through, but she could only smile through her haze of tears. "I'm fine," she whispered. "And so is our baby."

He whispered a sigh of thanks, then gathered her hair in his hand, tipping her head back until their eyes met. Then his mouth was on hers before she could tell him what she'd waited so long to tell him.

"You're forever mine," he murmured, cupping her face. "You've promised now, Doc, no backing out."

"Never," she vowed. *Forever his.* She liked the sound of that. "I love you, Ryan." Pulling his head back to hers, she kissed him with all the pent-up emotion she'd been holding back for too long. Needing more, her hands skimmed over his warm skin, hard muscle.

With a laughing moan he pulled away. "Oh, no, you don't. You can't seduce me here."

She batted her lashes, having planned exactly that. "Why not?"

"Because," he said with a wicked grin, "we've yet to make love properly, in a bed."

She thought about the boat, the table. "Maybe never a bed," she agreed, "but you have to admit, we did it properly."

He laughed again and pulled her off the deck into his moonlit bedroom. Yanking the covers down the bed, he turned to her, suddenly serious.

One by one he removed articles of her clothing, tossing them haphazardly around his room as if claiming it as her own territory. Gentle fingers touched the bandage on her head as she stood nude before him, quivering. It was almost frightening, how badly she needed him, how the weakness of it weighed her down.

"You've given me a hard time these past weeks, Kayla Davies." He feathered kisses over her jaw, her face. Knowing hands skimmed over her, leaving her aching for more. "You've aged me," he said solemnly. "It'll be your own fault if I can't perform now."

Then he tugged off his pants, leaving her breathless as she watched, admiring his rangy, tough body. His *hard* body. When he pulled her close, she felt him, hot and pulsing against her thigh, and despite herself, she smiled.

"You'll be fine," she assured him as he tumbled her down to the bed, covering her with his body, filling her as no other could.

"Mmmm," he said, tasting her skin. His voice came low, husky. "I guess you're right." He moved within her. "Tell me again, Kayla Davies, tell me how much you love me when you need me so badly you're shaking with it."

"I love you." She gasped as his teeth raked gently over an earlobe. His body thrust into hers again, creating a delicious, hazy friction.

"Again," he demanded, teasing his tongue over her heated skin, lifting her legs higher around him. "Tell me again."

But she was beyond words.

"That's okay," he murmured, stroking her into oblivion. "You're mine now. We have lots of time."

"Forever," she managed. "We have forever."

THE EDITORS'
CORNER

As the year draws to a close, we're delighted to bring you some Christmas cheer to warm and gladden your hearts. December's LOVESWEPTs will put a smile on your face and love on your mind, and when you turn that last page, you'll sigh longingly and maybe even wipe a few stray tears off your cheeks.

Rachel Lawrence and Sam Wyatt are setting off **FIREWORKS** in LOVESWEPT #862 by rising star RaeAnne Thayne. The last time Rachel left Whiskey Creek, she swore she'd never return. The only two people in the world who can force her to break her vow are her nephews. The problem is, Rachel and their father, Sam, can't stand each other. Now that Rachel's back in town, the sparks are flying. Sam can't understand why Rachel would take such a vested interest in the welfare of his sons—he just wants her to leave before he acts on the desire he feels for her. Rachel fears giving in to feelings for Sam she's harbored in her heart, harbored even before she lost her young husband in a brushfire. But when another brushfire threatens to claim the family ranch, will she forgive Sam for choosing duty over love? RaeAnne Thayne's tale sizzles with passion and is sure to keep you warm on even the coldest winter night!

In LOVESWEPT #863, Laura Taylor delivers **THE CHRISTMAS GIFT.** Former attorney Jack Howell thought his toughest cases were behind him, but when he returns to Kentucky to explore his new-found roots, he faces his most baffling case of all—an infant boy abandoned on his doorstep. Interior decorator Chloe McNeil's temper starts to simmer when Jack doesn't keep their appointment to discuss his new home. Maybe she's misjudged this man who so easily found a way into her heart. But when she drops by to give him a piece of her mind, she finds him knee-deep in diapers and formula. As Jack and Chloe care for the baby and try to keep Social Services from taking him away, will they discover that cherishing this child together is just the healing magic they need? Well-loved author Laura Taylor unites two wounded spirits during the season of Christmas harmony.

Remember Candy Johnson, Jen Casey's best friend in FOR LOVE OR MONEY, LOVESWEPT #849? Well, she's back with a hunk of her own in Kathy DiSanto's **HUNTER IN DISGUISE,** LOVE-SWEPT #864. Candy is sure there's more to George Price than his chunky glasses and ever-present pocket protector. For example, a chest and tush of Greek-god standards. And why would a gym teacher take out the soccer balls for the girls vs. guys volleyball match? And let's not forget about his penchant for B 'n' E (breaking and entering, that is). In the meantime, George has a problem all his own—trying to distract armchair detective Candy long enough to get his job done. George's less-than-debonair attributes prove to be easy enough to ignore as Candy gets to know the man beneath the look. Kathy DiSanto spins a breathless tale that's part wicked romp, part sexy suspense, and all pure pleasure!

Please welcome newcomer Catherine Mulvany to our Loveswept family as she presents **UPON A MIDNIGHT CLEAR,** LOVESWEPT #865. Alexandra Roundtree's obituary clearly stated she was no longer one of Brunswick, Oregon's, living citizens, but private investigator Dixon Yano is disabused of that notion when she comes walking into his agency in full disguise. Alex pleads with Dixon to help her find her would-be murderer, and after shots are fired through his window, Dixon decides to be her bodyguard. Soon, Dixon and Alex are forced into close quarters and intimate encounters. Even after her last romantic fiasco, Alex finds herself trusting in the man who has become her swashbuckling hero and lifesaver. Will Dixon cross the line between business and pleasure if it means risking his lady's life? Catherine Mulvany's first novel mixes up an explosively sensual cocktail that will touch and tantalize the soul!

Happy reading!

With warmest wishes,

Susann Brailey

Joy Abella

Susann Brailey   Joy Abella

Senior Editor   Administrative Editor

JILL SHALVIS

As some of you may already know, I am the original bookworm. My husband jokes that if I'm not eating or sleeping, I'm reading. As a mother of three very young children, that's not quite true, but close enough. I love to read, always have. I cut my teeth on the likes of Sandra Brown, Jayne Ann Krentz, and Nora Roberts — all incredibly gifted women. To me, writing always seemed like a dream . . . a wonderful, but impossible dream.

Then I realized that was silly. I tell my daughters they can do whatever they want for a living. Good advice. I took it. So when my dreams came true and Loveswept snapped up my stories, I danced down my hallway for weeks. I'm still dancing.

Not that much has changed. I still handle the very unglamorous chores of life. Except that now while I'm changing diapers, feeding hungry little mouths, and turning everyone's whites pink, I plot. I plot romance and laughter. I plot murder and mayhem. I love it. My family has gotten very used to me running for a piece of scratch paper every time an idea hits me. Or staring out the window for hours, hushing anyone who tries to talk to me while I'm "working." While the clouds puff merrily by, I'm plotting away.

I've had to put reading on a back burner for now, to be replaced by my new love of writing. But that's fine. I wouldn't change a thing. Luckily my husband cheerfully supports me in anything I do, so I write to my heart's content on a regular basis. What will I write in the future? Romance of course, because it's so wonderfully, deliciously satisfying.

Hope you find reading it as satisfying as I do writing it. Jill Shalvis, P.O. Box 1280, Chino, CA 91708-1280.

Loveswept®